When in Doubt Don't Chicken Out

The Travel Mishaps of Caity Shaw
Book Six

❧ ❧

Eliza Watson

When in Doubt Don't Chicken Out

BOOKS BY ELIZA WATSON

Nonfiction

Genealogy Tips & Quips

Fiction

A MAGS AND BIDDY GENEALOGY MYSTERY SERIES

How to Fake an Irish Wake (Book 1)
How to Snare a Dodgy Heir (Book 2)

THE TRAVEL MISHAPS OF CAITY SHAW SERIES

Flying by the Seat of My Knickers (Book 1)
Up the Seine Without a Paddle (Book 2)
My Christmas Goose Is Almost Cooked (Book 3)
My Wanderlust Bites the Dust (Book 4)
Live to Fly Another Day (Book 5)
When in Doubt Don't Chicken Out (Book 6)

WOMEN'S FICTION BOOKS

Kissing My Old Life Au Revoir

ROMANCE

Under Her Spell
Identity Crisis
'Til Death Do Us Part

WRITING YOUNG ADULT AS BETH WATSON

Getting a Life, Even if You're Dead

To my best friend, Lisa Hardel, for all the memories: the good, the bad, and the bogus—I couldn't resist referencing the 80s. Here's to many more!

ACKNOWLEDGMENTS

Thank you to all my Irish ancestors for inspiring my Caity Shaw series. Your homes, lives, and courage influenced many of the books' settings and storylines. In 2007, when I began my genealogy research, I had no idea it would lead to this incredible journey with Caity. She wouldn't have continued her travels if it wasn't for the brilliant fans who embarked on this adventure with us in *Flying by the Seat of My Knickers*. Thanks a mil! You are the best!

To all my friends and family—both in the US and Ireland—for believing in me and supporting my writing in so many ways. I would have given up years ago without your encouragement.

To Nikki Ford, Elizabeth Wright, and Meghan Lloyd for your in-depth feedback, helping to make this a stronger book. To Judy Watson for reading the book several times. To Dori Harrell for your fab editorial skills. To Chrissy Wolfe for your final proofreading tweaks. Thanks to you ladies, I can always publish a book with confidence. To Lyndsey Lewellen for another incredible cover and for capturing the spirit of Caity.

And to Amy Atwell at Author E.M.S. for a flawless interior format and for always promptly answering my many questions.

My Coffey Family Tree
Cheat Sheet

Great-grandparents
Patrick Coffey & Mary Flannery

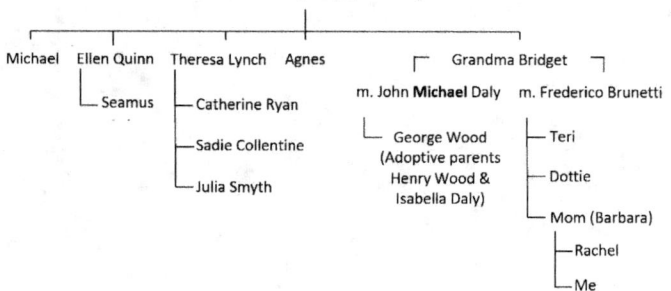

Michael   Ellen Quinn   Theresa Lynch   Agnes

— Seamus

— Catherine Ryan

— Sadie Collentine

— Julia Smyth

Grandma Bridget

m. John **Michael** Daly   m. Frederico Brunetti

— George Wood
(Adoptive parents
Henry Wood &
Isabella Daly)

— Teri

— Dottie

— Mom (Barbara)

— Rachel

— Me

CHAPTER ONE

"That wedding gown is bloody gorgeous." Zoe admired the satin dress, blinking back tears.

"I can't believe they're getting married." Fanny Bing stifled a dainty sob with a blue lace hanky.

"How long had they been going out?" Emily Ryan whispered.

"Off and on for the past six months," George told his aunt.

I shot my elderly uncle a suspicious glance. "I thought you didn't watch the TV show?"

George blushed. "Well, of course I had to watch a few episodes, seeing as they are filming here at my estate."

My Irish boyfriend, Declan, and I shared a smile. A playful glint in his dreamy blue eyes, he gave my hand a gentle squeeze. My shoulders relaxed for the first time that day.

Thomas's nervous gaze narrowed on his floral arrangements on the fireplace mantel at the front of the salon. "I should have added some Achillea." The gardener was hoping the wedding's exposure would get him a spread in English garden magazines.

The bride and groom, Caroline and Lawrence, were characters on *Sunnyvale*, a horrible, yet popular, soap opera I'd been sucked into watching on numerous occasions. The show was filming its much-anticipated wedding episode at my uncle George Wood's estate in Dalwick, England. I was in attendance because my sister, Rachel, the event planner, had been stranded at O'Hare airport. Not because I was hoping the bride dumped the jerk at the altar.

The blond actress sashayed down the open wooden staircase, her blue eyes gazing lovingly at her future husband—a handsome thirty-year-old Scottish gent— waiting by the unlit fireplace. The couple had eloped to a romantic stately home. The only guests, we huddled in the foyer entrance and watched the filming, as quiet as mice. Hopefully, a little critter wouldn't scamper across the salon during the ceremony. We waited in anticipation for the bride to walk down the aisle, lined with an array of Thomas's prize-winning flowers.

The processional song began playing.

The actress's refined nose scrunched at a foul odor filling the air.

Zoe's top lip curled back. "What's that wretched stench?" My best friend, and Declan's sister, sniffed the front of her emerald-green dress, then swept her long blond ponytail under her nose to block the smell.

"Septic tank backed up, is it?" Declan asked.

Fanny covered her nose with her hanky.

"Cut!" the director yelled. "What the bloody hell is that smell?"

A dozen cast and crew members peered over at us. As if *we* were responsible for the stench.

But they were right. It seemed to be coming from our direction...

A loud belch filled the air.

Everyone's gazes darted to Mac, lying innocently under an antique wooden credenza behind us. Egg salad matted the tan fur around my Irish terrier's mouth. He'd gotten into the crew's food! Declan had planned to take him out for the day, but he'd confessed last minute to wanting to watch the filming. Mac had been behaving, until now.

The director called for a thirty-minute break and gave us a stern warning to get rid of the smell ASAP. The cast and crew headed outside for some fresh air.

Zoe gave Mac a sympathetic smile. "Not in great form, are ya, fella?"

I was one major bill away from falling back into serious debt; however, my anger quickly evolved into panic. "Are eggs or mayo toxic to dogs?"

"I don't think so." Declan Googled it on his phone. "But it obviously isn't doing him any good."

We'd all signed a confidentiality agreement not to disclose the filming location until the episode aired in three weeks. We now agreed not to mention Mac's mishap to Rachel. She was stressed out enough, unable to be here.

Hanky still to her nose, Fanny went in search of air freshener. Emily, Thomas, and George escaped with her. I knelt down in my fancy white lace dress and grabbed ahold of Mac, limp as a rag doll. I slid him out from under the table, causing him to pass more gas.

"Jaysus." Declan scooped Mac up and held him against the front of his white oxford shirt and black suit jacket. "I'll take him out back and hook his leash to the clothesline. Fresh air will do him good."

"I'll see what's in the bathroom cabinet for gas and indigestion that might be safe for dogs," Zoe said.

"See if there's a lint brush." I plucked Mac's tan fur from my dress.

We'd dressed as wedding guests since the show was providing us a promo shot of the couple and one with them and our staff. I'd even flat-ironed my auburn hair and allowed Zoe to swap out my tinted lip gloss for red lipstick, which I never wore. I'd borrowed her fancy red hat with a cluster of maple leaves on one side—a replica of the hat Kate, Duchess of Cambridge, had worn on a visit to Canada. A present from Declan this past Christmas.

I bolted into the oak-paneled library to check on the crew's food. First, I navigated around an eclectic array of couches, love seats, and chairs, which provided seating for fifty attendees at the estate's art-mystery events. I opened the tall windows, giving the cast and crew in the garden a wave. I flew over to the food buffet on an antique credenza. Pieces of a broken china platter were scattered across the worn oriental rug, along with scraps of bread licked clean of egg salad.

A growl vibrated at the back of my throat. I dropped to the floor to clean up the mess and stared into the beady eyes of the mouse we'd been trying to capture for the past week. It held a half-eaten white chocolate button, its cheeks bulging. The top request on the actress's long list of demands.

"Shit!" I yelled.

The mouse scampered off.

I sprang up with a handful of buttons. Everyone in the garden was staring at me. Smiling, I gave them a flutter wave.

Declan flew into the room and eyed the mess. "Jaysus."

"This was the last of the buttons. I didn't think such a skinny woman would eat more than a bag of chocolate."

Declan studied the buttons in my hand. "They're grand." He dumped them in a teacup on the table.

"We can't do that."

"Do you want to be telling that diva you're out of her sweets?"

I shook my head.

Luckily, Mac hadn't touched the ham and tuna sandwiches or the baked goods. The actress had hired Fanny to bake her yummy scones for an afternoon tea fundraiser. Fanny had hopes that her baked goods would soon be served in England's finest tea shops.

Declan cleaned up the mess while I replenished the egg salad. We returned to the salon as if nothing had happened.

Fanny was saturating the room with a vanilla-scented spray. "Already smelling good as new." She let out a contented sigh, gazing at the wedding set past the filming and lighting equipment. "It's so romantic."

George's smile faded into a frown. "But this shouldn't have been the first wedding to take place here. It should have been..." He peered tenderly at Fanny, enveloping her hands in his. Her breath caught in her throat; her pale-blue eyes widened with anticipation. "Fanny, my dear, will you do me the honor of becoming my wife?"

Fanny nodded enthusiastically. "I do." She giggled like a young girl. "Or rather, I *will*, and then I *do*."

A few months ago, Fanny had given up hope of having a relationship with George when he'd announced he was moving to the Canary Islands. He'd been trying to escape his past, rather than Fanny. Now he and Fanny had a future together.

George's eyes watered. "I don't deserve you, but I love you very much."

"Don't speak such nonsense," Fanny said, her voice cracking with emotion. "I love you. And the name Mrs. George Wood."

The couple sealed their engagement with a kiss, embracing.

I glanced at Declan through a glassy-eyed haze. He smiled at me, and my chest fluttered.

"Congratulations." Emily gave them a hug. Her tall, slender figure towered over her nephew and Fanny. She snagged a flute of apple cider from a table.

Everyone joined in, downing the beverage.

I leaned toward Zoe. "Could you please get more glasses of cider before they need the props for the champagne toast?"

She nodded and fled to the kitchen.

"Your bouquet must include bright-blue cornflowers, some nigella in soft blue hues..."

While Thomas envisioned the florals, I gave my uncle George and his new fiancée each a big hug. "I'm so happy for you guys."

Fanny smiled at George. "When shall it take place?"

He glanced over at me. "Your mother, Teri, and

Dottie will be visiting in five weeks. I'd like to include my newfound sisters in the joyous occasion." He looked at Fanny for approval.

"Sounds lovely."

"You and Rachel must attend as family members so you can enjoy the day," George told me. "We'll hire a wedding planner."

I shook my head. "No way will Rachel entrust your big day to some stranger."

"You must attend as more than merely a family member," Fanny said. "Please say you'll be my maid of honor."

George smiled in agreement. "Yes, it's thanks to you I finally came to my senses."

I fought back tears once again, not wanting raccoon eyes for the promo shot. "I'd love to."

George placed a hand on Thomas's shoulder. "And of course, you shall be by my side that day."

The gardener nodded. "I'd be proud."

"It'll be an intimate wedding of close family and friends," Fanny said. "My dress will be pale blue, and a matching vest and bow tie for George."

Fanny currently wore a blue floral dress, and George a green tweed jacket and tan slacks. Even the woman's white hair had a faint blue tint. George had a refined air about him but preferred a casual look and rarely got spiffed up.

"You must wear my mother's brooch," George said.

George's biological mother—my grandma Bridget Coffey Brunetti—and my mother had both worn the piece of silver jewelry with emerald-colored stones for their weddings.

Zoe returned from the kitchen and pulled me off to the side. "There's only enough cider for one glass. I found apple cider vinegar. I could add a bit to water."

"Sounds good."

"What if it doesn't bubble like champagne?"

"I'll blow bubbles through a straw before they film it."

Zoe flew back to the kitchen.

I smiled at George and Fanny. "I'm going to call Rachel so she can start planning the wedding." I headed into the foyer.

Having only five weeks to organize the wedding might push Rachel over the edge she'd been teetering on. The soap opera hadn't confirmed the filming location until two weeks ago, not wanting it to leak to the media. As if it were a royal wedding. So she'd had to scramble to plan the event from Milwaukee. Then she'd been stranded at O'Hare for several days because of severe weather around the US. The first available flight would have gotten her here tomorrow, so she'd given up and gone home.

This meant I'd had to be in England earlier than expected for the furniture delivery and set change. Red upholstered antique furnishings replaced the flying monkey table and Fanny's blue wingback chair in the salon. Being a savvy contract negotiator, Rachel had insisted that the show's furniture remain at the estate for future events. Robert Daly—the show's location scout and no relation to George—had been so impressed with Declan's reproductions of the estate's stolen artwork that he'd paid to have them framed. Hopefully, the TV exposure would make Declan some sales on the estate's website.

I FaceTimed my sister. She was wearing her boyfriend Gerry's oversized red rugby jersey for pajamas, her brown hair was in a lopsided ponytail, and smeared mascara framed her blue eyes. I told her about George and Fanny's engagement, swearing her to secrecy until they called Mom following the filming.

"That's it. I quit," she said.

"You can't quit. George and Fanny need your help planning the wedding."

"I'm quitting Brecker, not the estate job."

Panic raced through me.

I'd undoubtedly get stuck with Rachel's meetings until her position was filled. I was part time at Flanagan's beer but contracted by Brecker—my company's owner and Rachel's employer. If I took on Rachel's programs, I wouldn't have time to plan the Daly clan gathering in two weeks here at George's. An event that would bring Dalys together from around the world and bring me some genealogy business.

"The transatlantic commute is killing me." Rachel let out an exhausted groan. "Not to mention I've blown through most of my frequent flyer miles."

Over the past few months, Rachel had flown to England for six art-mystery events and a garden party. I'd executed two events when she hadn't made it back due to work or weather.

"Once this episode airs, we'll be slammed with events, especially weddings," she said. "Fans are going to want tours of the filming location. I'm planning afternoon tea three days a week, maybe every day in the summer."

What was this "we" thing? I already had *three* jobs. Flanagan's, executing art-mystery events here on weekends, and a fledgling genealogy business. And if Rachel quit Brecker, I'd be picking up her work.

Whoever thought *I'd* be picking up *Rachel's* slack?

"I won't need to wait a year to take a wage," Rachel said. "I can start now. It won't be much since the estate is in such massive debt, but I can live between Gerry's in Dublin and George's. I'm handing in my notice tomorrow."

"I didn't know you and Gerry had discussed living together."

"Going to be living together, are ya?" Declan materialized next to me.

Rachel beamed with enthusiasm. "Can you believe it?"

"Right, then, that's grand." Declan's strained smile faded, and he walked off.

Declan's and my living situation was a sore subject. He stayed at my studio apartment in Dublin when he wasn't traveling for work or we weren't spending weekends at George's, but we hadn't officially moved in together. Living together was a huge step. Until three months ago, we'd only seen each other every four to six weeks for a few days. Declan wanted us to move into a larger apartment and split the rent. I refused to give up my place over Coffey's pub. I'd never find such an incredible deal again. Not that I was pessimistic about our relationship. However, being able to stand on my own was an empowering feeling after escaping my emotionally abusive ex-boyfriend.

I finished the call and joined everyone in the library, except Zoe, drinking tea and discussing wedding plans. I plopped down onto a tan brocade upholstered chair.

"A few months ago, we wouldn't have been able to consider holding the wedding in the house," Fanny said. "That charcoal really has done wonders to freshen up the place."

"Charcoal?" Emily said.

Fanny explained my mom's method of using charcoal briquettes to remove moisture from the stately home this past spring. The damp and musty interior had been at least partially responsible for George ending up in the hospital with pneumonia.

Emily nodded with interest. "I will have to give that a try. I might never be able to get the musty smell out of my family home in Killybog. My friend Margaret used to stop by every few days and open up the house, but she's no longer able to drive. It's difficult for me to make it over there often from Dublin. The place needs to be lived in, or I fear it may begin crumbling to the ground. But you can't trust just anyone in your home."

"You could trust *me* there," Declan said.

My gaze darted to Declan, who avoided my shocked look.

"Are you saying you'd like to be the caretaker?" Emily arched an intrigued brow. "To live there?"

Declan nodded. "I could whip it back into shape. Could paint murals on your walls if you like." A glint of inspiration sparkled in his blue eyes.

If Declan moved to Killybog, we'd never see each other. And what would Grandma think of him living in the Dalys' stately home where the English landowners had looked down the hill on their Irish Coffey tenants' humble stone cottage? A rift between the two families had caused Grandma and her first husband, Michael

Daly, to become estranged from their families following their marriage.

"Sounds like a perfect position for you," George said.

Having both Daly and Coffey genes—making George my *half*-uncle—he wouldn't have an issue with Declan living in his father's childhood home.

"Would you be able to break the lease on your current flat?" Emily asked.

"Don't have one. When I'm not working in a hotel, I crash at Caity's or my parents'."

Crashed? He considered staying at my place *crashing*?

"You mentioned that you paint. My peach room would make a lovely studio, with its sun exposure."

"Can you help me get more scones?" I asked Declan.

We headed into the kitchen as Zoe exited with a tray of champagne flutes. Noticing our serious looks, she kept walking.

I spun around toward Declan. "If you live at Emily's, I'll never see you."

"I'll still come to Dublin one night a week, and we'll see each other on weekends. Or you could move into Emily's with me." He cocked a brow, challenging me.

A forty-five-minute rush-hour commute to Dublin would be a nightmare. Not to mention I didn't own a car. And I still had to go into Flanagan's office twice a week. My bus commute provided me time to plan the Daly clan gathering in two weeks. He knew I couldn't move to Emily's.

Was that why he was asking me to?

"Is this about Rachel and Gerry moving in together?" Or Caroline and Lawrence's wedding and George and Fanny's engagement?

A baffled look creased his brow. "No. It's about me living between hotels, your place, here, and my parents'. Emily's house is near Dublin, and that peach room sounds like a brilliant studio. Your flat is too cramped and dark for painting. Only painting a few weekends a month here or at my parents' isn't enough. And if I can't paint at your place, what am I supposed to do? Join your neighbor's ukulele group?"

I agreed the ukulele group was no longer as quaint as when I'd first moved in. "My grandma will turn over in her grave if you live in the Daly house."

Declan ran a frustrated hand through his short, wavy brown hair. "I thought you'd be grand with me living by your granny's house so you could visit anytime, along with seeing your cousins Sadie and Seamus. I respect the fact that you don't want to officially live together, so respect the fact that the arrangement isn't working for me."

Was he referring to our *living* arrangement or *us*?

Feeling light-headed, I grabbed a glass of water from the counter and took a large gulp. My lips puckered, and a sour, acidic taste filled my mouth. Zoe's apple cider vinegar concoction. I dumped it in the sink. I found a lone bottle of cider ale at the back of the fridge.

"That's been in there forever," Declan said. "It's probably shite."

"It's better than the alternative, and it has bubbles."

Declan placed a calming hand on my arm. "Things will be fine. Besides, we owe Emily after she managed to get your citizenship expedited."

Thanks to Emily, my citizenship had been finalized three weeks ago. Otherwise I'd have been deported and living with my parents in Milwaukee, in my old bedroom with pink walls and a pink lacy comforter.

"You can't blame Emily for something her father did eighty years ago," Declan said. "And the Coffeys surely hated the Dalys just as much, if not more."

Rational or not, Declan moving into the Daly house seemed disrespectful to Grandma's memory. And a bit disrespectful to me that he hadn't at least consulted me on the idea. I was ready to say that when the film crew's voices carried in from the salon.

Fanny and George were getting married. Rachel and Gerry would be shacking up. Declan would be living at Emily's stately home, while Mac and I would be stuck in a tiny apartment. Not to mention George's estate, Fanny's scones, Declan's paintings, Thomas's flowers, and Rachel's career were all about to take off after the wedding episode aired. Everyone was moving forward with their lives thanks to me, *except* for me.

Why did a step forward for me—wanting to be able to stand on my own—have to be a step backward for Declan and me?

CHAPTER
TWO

The following morning, I entered my Dublin studio apartment with a bag of scones from a quaint bakery down the street. They were tasty but not nearly as delish as Fanny's strawberry chocolate chip ones. Mac's chin rested on the edge of the yellow duvet-covered bed, his sad brown eyes watching Declan toss belongings into a box.

A sick feeling tossed my tummy.

When I'd left my ex, I'd thrown crap into boxes, suitcases, garbage bags, any available containers so I'd be gone before he'd gotten home from work. I'd taken a painting that he'd claimed was his, giving him a "valid" excuse to stalk me.

My gaze darted to the painting of Declan's parents' house hanging on the wall next to my portrait, which he'd sketched in Prague. I let out a relieved sigh he hadn't packed them.

An art easel wedged in the corner displayed a blank canvas. And a single window in the kitchenette facing an alley provided minimal natural lighting. He was right. Emily's place was ideal for painting, except for the feud between the Dalys and my Coffeys. Granted, living in such cramped quarters was a bit trying at times, but I'd had no clue he'd jump at the chance to move out.

A flip of the switch and the plastic pitcher plugged into the wall by the small dorm-size fridge soon started whistling, steam rising from its spout. I selected two teacups from my collection and let the tea brew. Bags of Taytos filled a bowl on the counter. "You should take some of these Taytos and the peanut butter and jelly so you have something for dinner."

"I bought all that for you."

Declan did a better job than I did at remembering to pick up my favorite foods when he went shopping.

I nearly burst into tears over Taytos.

"You Are My Sunshine" played on a ukulele in my neighbor Fiona's apartment. Her new student had been attempting to master the song for the past few weeks.

Mac howled every time the person hit a wrong chord.

I pounded on the wall. "Stop with that song!"

Silence.

Declan looked freaked out by my outburst.

I'd never screamed at a neighbor before. I was a woman on the edge. As if Fiona was responsible for Declan moving out. I hoped I hadn't given the elderly instructor a heart attack.

"Sorry!" I yelled out.

The music resumed.

I rolled my eyes.

"You should take the bed," I told Declan. "It's yours."

He'd bought me the white bed frame and matching dresser as a housewarming gift. So the three of us didn't have to sleep together on the red couch his parents had given me. Mac was a total bed hog.

"Emily's bedrooms are furnished. Besides, I'll still be sleeping here once in a while, and you need a bed."

Once in a while?

Declan peered over at Mac, who was depressed as usual after returning from George's sprawling estate to our tiny apartment. And he sensed that Declan was leaving. This morning he'd refused to eat or go for a walk. His tummy might also still be upset from the plateful of egg salad sandwiches.

"Cheer up, little fella," Declan said. "You'll be staying with me this week while your mum's gone."

I cringed at the thought of the upcoming Kerry meeting with my nasty coworker Gemma. Yet it was a good sign that Declan wanted joint custody of Mac.

Declan gave Mac a comforting pat. "Ya might even find some sheep on the road that need herding back into a field."

Mac's ears perked up as if he understood.

Thanks to George's nasty cousin Enid, Mac had found his calling as a sheepherder. However, the new lock on George's gate had prevented Enid from letting any more sheep loose on the estate's grounds. Another thing that had thrown Mac into a funk. He'd lost his sense of purpose and had no goals.

Speaking of sheep, Declan's blue wool sweater lay on top of a pile of clothes in his open suitcase. The sweater I'd been wearing since staying at George's chilly estate in March.

"You're taking that sweater?"

"Thought you wouldn't be needing it. Despite pissing rain, it's been warm out."

"I just wore it two days ago. You saw me wear it. And it's only in the fifties right now. Are you taking the paintings you gave me also?" I gestured toward the artwork on the wall.

He snatched up the sweater. "That's grand. Keep it."

"It feels like we're splitting our belongings."

"I thought it'd be best moving today so ya didn't come home from Kerry to my stuff gone, as if I'd left ya in the middle of the night. But maybe I should have waited." Declan's gaze softened. He draped the sweater around my shoulders and grasped the sleeves, pulling me toward him. "This will be grand, Caity. I'll be able to pursue my art and eventually stop traveling. Not gonna make five thousand off every painting like I did at the art-mystery event this spring. And you can focus more on your genealogy business."

And focus less on *him*?

He grabbed a small cardboard box off the desk and handed it to me. "A present."

I opened it to find the business cards I'd created online. I hadn't placed the order, unable to get a professional look without lying about being a certified genealogist. When I'd worked as an on-site travel staff, Declan had always said, "Fake it till you make it." Yet I couldn't fake finding dead people.

I smiled. "Thanks. They're perfect."

His gaze narrowed. "Which do ya fear more, failure or success?"

"Who would be afraid of success?" The fear of failing at another job was almost paralyzing.

"Then why can't ya commit to it?"

Were we talking about my genealogy business or our relationship?

"Nicholas's death was brutal, but you'll find another mentor."

I'd met Nicholas Turney, a historian and Declan's parents' neighbor, last Christmas when he'd helped me with my Coffey family research. He'd loaned me two genealogy books when I'd taken on my first clients, Bernice and Gracie. He'd set me on the path to becoming a genealogist and given me confidence. He'd also helped me search for Grandma's birth record, which was required for me to obtain Irish citizenship. I'd been in a bit of a funk since his death last month.

"How's the website coming along?"

I had a domain name.

"Nigel, Bernice, and Gretchen gave me testimonials for it. Who'd have ever thought Gretchen would give me a rave review?"

Gretchen and I had become archenemies while working together as travel staff. She'd been jealous of Declan's and my friendship, and she was a raging bitch. After bonding during a horrific meeting in Prague, she'd hired me to research her paternal ancestry. I'd discovered her grandfather was born in Hungary rather than Germany, enabling her to obtain dual citizenship and one day own a mountain cottage in Bavaria.

"Bernice should give you a brilliant one after ya found rellies for her and Gracie to visit in Scotland."

"And I'd have had another client if that Scottish Coffey couple hadn't been impatient and hired someone else." I heaved a sigh. "This whole starting-my-own-business thing isn't easy. I've known all *three* of my clients and been up front that I'm a total rookie. So if I didn't succeed, they'd know what they were getting into. I can't ask new clients to cut me some slack. They won't hire me. Even if I don't admit I'm a newbie, being so young, people will assume I'm inexperienced."

Declan tucked a stray clump of hair behind my ear, his fingers lingering, warm against my skin. "Dye your hair gray."

I smiled, the tension in my body relaxing. "It doesn't feel right charging the same as certified genealogists. But if I charge less, people might wonder why. And I can't afford less." My chest tightened at the mere thought of bill collectors once again stalking me. "Besides, I'll get a ton of work from this clan gathering. Sixty-four people have registered. I don't want to take on clients before it, then be too busy for more. One of the event's highlights is having access to a genealogist. So I'll have to have my website done before the event."

Declan looked unconvinced.

As nervous as Rachel was over the estate's event business exploding once the soap opera episode aired, I was nervous that my genealogy business would explode after the clan gathering. But unlike my sister, I'd become overwhelmed, incapable of handling the influx of clients. Especially if I was working my job and Rachel's.

For the first time in my life, was I afraid of *success*?

My cell phone dinged the arrival of an e-mail. A welcome interruption from Declan's interrogation.

Fanny said she and her friend Mary were excited to attend their first hen party. Fanny wanted to break tradition and have the bachelorette party after the wedding so my mom and her sisters could attend. If I could please keep that in mind while planning it.

I'd only attended one bachelorette party. Two if I counted the one last fall on a Seine dinner cruise when I'd been seated with a hen party from England. The women had resembled beauty-pageant contestants in fancy dresses with sashes that read *Bride-to-Be* and *Ellie's Bridesmaids.* Fanny wouldn't expect a party in Paris, would she? And I wasn't expected to pay for it, was I?

Yet I had to make it a memorable event for Fanny. What kind of bachelorette party did I organize for a group of mostly elderly women?

⁂

We stopped at Coffey's pub to tell my landlord, Gerry, we wouldn't be around this week, including Mac. Gerry Coffey—fortyish with dark hair, blue eyes, and a five-o'clock shadow—stood behind the long wooden bar serving two old men focused on a large-screen TV on the wall. Rather than a brutal rugby match, they were watching a shouting match between two characters on *Sunnyvale.*

"Thought you didn't watch the show?" I asked Gerry. The pub owner glanced over at me. "Seeing as

Rachel is binge-watching it, thought it'd be best I know a bit about the show. Can't walk down the street without seeing it advertised. Hell, had a poster 'bout it in the lad's loo at McCabe's."

Despite the show's confidentiality agreement, Rachel had told Gerry about the filming. She'd refused to lie about a last-minute trip to England when he'd known there was no event scheduled. The past three months they'd only seen each other when Rachel flew over to execute events in England, where Gerry met up with her.

A chalkboard behind the bar advertised specialty drinks. *Hitched*—a fruity-flavored martini. *Ditched*—a drink with three shots of hard liquor. The *Sunnyvale* promo tagline was *Is he getting hitched or ditched?* As in, would Caroline marry or break up with Lawrence? Curious minds wanted to know.

I gestured to the sign. "Cute."

One of the older men turned to Gerry. "Be ditching the bloody eejit, she will."

"Ya never know," the other man said. "Even the actors mightn't be knowing. My wife said back when Caroline's parents were married, the show filmed two endings so even the cast and crew couldn't be leaking it to the media."

Gerry, Declan, and I exchanged panicked looks.

"Right, then," Gerry said. "Figure the drinks be helping create hype so you and Rachel will have loads of events. Which ya will. I certainly won't be telling her otherwise."

Yet what if the guy was right? TV shows often filmed alternate endings for season and series finales. This was a season finale before the show took a one-month hiatus. Rachel, George, and everyone involved would be devastated if the bastard Lawrence was ditched rather than hitched at the estate.

Starting to sweat, I pushed up the sleeves of Declan's blue wool sweater. I'd put it on to prove a point, and to be wrapped in his woodsy cologne and the soft, snuggly fabric. It was my comfort sweater.

Gerry eyed Declan. "So ya going to be caretaker for a rellie of Caity's uncle, are ya? Rachel says it's a brilliant position."

Unlike me, it hadn't bothered my sister when I'd told her Declan was going to live in the Daly house. Yet she hadn't experienced firsthand my emotional journey to discovering Grandma's family home. The heart-wrenching story of Grandma's estrangement from her family, then being widowed and abandoning Uncle George with her husband's cousin Isabella Daly Wood in England. Following all that she emigrated alone from Ireland to America.

Gerry gave me a nod. "Suppose you're here to inform me that ya will no longer be needing the flat."

Declan's body went rigid next to me. "She's staying here."

"I, ah, need to live in Dublin for work," I said. "And to have access to the archives for genealogy research." I hadn't yet been to the archives, but I would once my business took off.

Gerry poured orange juice into a glass with vodka, mixing a drink. "Does Rachel fancy orange juice?"

I shook my head. "Too high in carbs."

"Doing a Tesco run before she moves here."

I rattled off Rachel's favorite foods. Gerry jotted them down on the back of a Guinness coaster.

"What about toothpaste? No need for two kinds. Can be sharing a tube." The thought of sharing dental hygiene products put a goofy grin on Gerry's face. "Sorry. I know I seem a bit mad about the whole thing, but I really want this to work. Not just the living together, but our relationship. I've never felt this way 'bout a woman."

He was sounding a bit mushy. He wasn't going to pop the question, was he? What if Gerry and Rachel were the third couple married at the estate, when Declan and I were no longer even living together? When had my sister become the spontaneous, reckless one and I'd become more conservative and cautious?

However, I was happy for Rachel. Her previous boyfriends were boring businessmen. Like Brandon, the stockbroker who'd offered to help me invest. When I'd jokingly asked him how long it would take to turn ten bucks into a million, he'd done the math in his head and advised me of the power of compound interest. In hindsight, I should have taken him up on his offer to manage my money.

My phone rang. Mom.

"I better take this." I stepped outside into a downpour and ducked under the store's awning next door. Not a touristy area, a few locals were in raincoats or under umbrellas, walking dogs or trudging along in desperate need of caffeine.

Mom wasn't going to be happy, but I explained that Declan had taken the caretaker job at the Daly house.

"How nice. What an ideal spot for him to paint."

"Ideal as in he won't be living with me?"

Three months ago, when Mom had visited, she'd made not-so-subtle remarks about how we shouldn't rush into living together. She'd thought Declan was witty, charming, and handsome, just not roommate material so early on in our relationship.

"I thought you weren't *living* together? Why are you so upset? Is he moving out because you two had an argument?"

"What would Grandma think of this? After the way the Dalys treated our family."

"That was Emily's father and a hundred years ago. I think it's time to let bygones be bygones. I'm sure my mother would be thrilled over George and Fanny's engagement. When George called with the news, Fanny asked my blessing to wear my mother's brooch. How sweet is that? Of course, I gave it to her. I wish I could be there to help plan it..."

Why was I the only one bothered by Declan living in the Daly home?

A bus rumbled past with a *Sunnyvale* poster of Caroline and Lawrence plastered on the side. A tidal wave of water splashed up from the street, drenching me. Declan's soaked wool sweater clung to my body. I needed a drink.

Hitched or *Ditched?* I wasn't sure.

CHAPTER THREE

"That bloke is scary as bloody hell." Zoe's blue-eyed gaze narrowed on the gilded-framed painting of Emily's grandfather hanging on the hallway's dark-green wall. "Even if he smiled, he'd look crazed, with those freaky dark eyes. Looks right pissed off, he does."

"About us being in his house, no doubt." I smiled at the thought of making that horrible man roll over in his grave.

"The cobwebs on the frame add to the creepy factor. Maybe the painting's supposed to ward off evil. Like gargoyles on churches. Those beastly looking yokes supposedly protect the church from evil. Yet they're cute as kittens compared to this fella."

Besides the cobwebs, spiders, and dead flies everywhere, the house smelled mustier than it had at Christmastime. The loss of Emily's caretaker had definitely taken a toll on the place.

"With that pasty-white skin, he obviously didn't work outdoors."

"I'm sure he led a pampered life as a wealthy landlord. Except, of course, when he was targeted by angry tenants, who mistakenly shot his sister instead of him."

I wasn't certain my Coffeys hadn't been involved in the assassination plot.

"Too bad their aim was shite."

Mac growled at the painting, sounding more ferocious than he looked in the pink bunny sweater Zoe had knitted him for Easter. Unlike his green St. Patrick's Day's tutu, a few hours in a sweater and he was itching to get out of it. I'd had him wear it for Zoe's sake. He'd better appreciate the fact that I'd refused Zoe's request for him to model her dog apparel at a craft show. I'd witnessed her poor cat, Quigley, wearing the latest cat fashions at a show. His expression had made Grumpy Cat look downright perky.

The man's spooky eyes seemed to follow us down the hallway, raising the hairs on my arms.

We joined Declan in the orangish-peach room where he was setting up an easel near the front window— overlooking my Coffeys' home down the hill. More portraits filled the walls, along with paintings of horses, some with dapper-looking gents in red riding outfits. Zoe plopped down on the green velvet couch with ornately carved wood trim. I sat next to her in a matching chair.

She picked up one of the red floral china cups displayed on a silver tray. "Fancy a spot of tea?" she said in a refined accent, holding the cup's handle with her pinky pointing out.

"Emily gave me a cup." Yet accepting a Daly teacup

was much different than living in the house. "It gives me a sense of satisfaction that I have a cup from the family collection, which old man Daly made sure my grandma never inherited."

Declan perched a blank canvas on the easel. "I need to get started on Rachel's painting."

My sister had hired him to paint a wedding portrait of Caroline and Lawrence to hang over the fireplace in George's library.

"If Caity won't be moving in, I'll certainly stay here." Zoe relaxed back on the couch. "Quigley would love sunning himself in those massive windowsills." A strong breeze sucked the cream-colored drapes out the screenless, partially open windows. "And I could make loads of decorating suggestions, like getting rid of the scary family portrait in the hallway."

After recently graduating from the university, Zoe had landed a supervisor position at a décor and gift shop in Mullingar that promoted Irish artisans—selling Declan's paintings and Zoe's knitted pet apparel.

I shot Zoe a disapproving glance for bringing up our living situation.

Sorry, she mouthed.

"Planning on joining a dart league at Carter's, are ya?" Zoe asked.

"Not sure. Already joined one at my mate Peter Molloy's pub. Will see if I have time for two nights out a week."

What about coming to Dublin and seeing me during the week?

"Ack, forgot my phone in the car." Zoe sprang from the couch and zipped out of the room.

My gaze narrowed on Declan. "What will you do with Mac when you're at Molloy's? He'll destroy this place if you leave him here alone. I can't afford to be replacing Emily's antiques."

"I'll bring him with."

"A pub isn't an appropriate place for Mac to hang out."

"We take him to Carter's all the time."

True. The pub owners, Des and Mags, even carried his favorite dog treats.

"Mac will be grand," Declan said. "If not, maybe it's time to kennel train him."

If staying in my tiny studio apartment threw my dog into a funk, what would being confined in a cage do to him?

"I'm not sure how I feel about Mac in a kennel."

Having heard his name, Mac trotted into the room, a lace doily hanging from his mouth.

I clapped my hands. "Mac. Drop that!"

With an irked look, he trotted back out, doily in mouth.

I really needed to read my *Dog Training for Dummies* book.

We followed Mac down the hallway. He reached the front door as Zoe was opening it to come inside. He bolted out.

"Shite!" Declan yelled, flying out the door.

We joined Declan in hot pursuit. Mac raced down the tree-lined dirt drive. My heart pounded. Yet rather than heading toward the open gate, Mac made a detour toward the Coffeys' stone cottage covered with a rusted metal roof. He disappeared in the overgrown grass.

We arrived at the house out of breath, panting. Mac was sitting at the weathered green wooden door hanging crooked on rusted hinges. The doily gone from his mouth.

"Where the hell is the doily?" I said.

Our gazes darted to the field of tall grass leading back up to Emily's.

"I'll look for it." Zoe went off in search of the vintage lace.

"Mac, that was very naughty."

He pawed at the cottage's door, whimpering.

A scratching noise responded on the other side, followed by a loud squawking.

Mac stepped back, eying the door with curiosity.

"What the hell?" Declan muttered.

We peeked through a glassless window into the dark dwelling. A hen stood perched on a brick placed on the dirt floor in front of the door to keep it closed. Its plumage was brown with an orangish-gold-colored neck and a bright-red comb. The bird continued squawking.

"How did it get in there?" I asked.

"Chickens can fly a few feet off the ground. Just not any distance."

"Then why doesn't it fly back out?"

The hen once again scratched at the door.

"I'll hold Mac while you let it out." I grasped ahold of the dog's collar.

Declan eased open the door.

The hen waddled out, beak in the air.

Mac drew back his head, growling. He went wild, jerking free from my hold. Rather than attacking the chicken, he raced off, past Zoe in the field, toward Emily's house. What had happened to the fearless sheepherder mere months ago at George's?

The hen disappeared out the gate and down the road as if it had places to go and people to see.

A bark filled the air. Mac sat on the front stoop at Emily's Georgian-style stone house, impatiently waiting to be let in.

"Mac can't stay here if he's going to eat all the lace doilies and run away. You need to keep that gate closed. I mean, seriously. You're going to need to pack away all of Emily's valuables. And you better put a gate in that hallway so he can't escape again. We might never find him."

"Then train him," Declan said calmly, despite my rant. "What's *really* wrong? Why are ya so upset about me staying here?"

"Not asking my opinion about moving here was disrespectful," I blurted out. "It's like something—" I snapped my mouth shut.

Declan's eyes widened with shock. "*Andy* would have done?"

"I didn't say that." But I almost had. After months of barely thinking about that bastard, I'd allowed him to once again mess with my mind. Declan was charming, considerate, loving, everything Andy wasn't. Yet I was upset over this one thing that had reminded me of my ex? However, I'd promised myself I'd never let a man disrespect me again.

"Last year at this time I was lying on my parents' couch eating frosting out of a container, not showering for weeks. I refuse to be that person again."

"As if *I'd* be making ya that person again."

Declan's wounded expression made my heart ache.

"I'd like to think maybe I have something to do with how well you're faring. Or at least how well I *thought* ya were faring."

"Of course, you've helped me recover. I never thought I'd ever kiss a guy again, let alone have a relationship. I've made huge progress. I just need some time to prove I can stand on my own."

Declan arched a questioning brow. "On your *own*?"

"Sorry. That's not what I meant."

"Are ya sure?"

"Yes, I'm sure. I just meant I want to be self-sufficient, not without you. I don't ever want to be without you."

Zoe joined us, tossing her hands in the air. "Can't find the bloody yoke. Maybe Mac ate it."

"If he did, he better poop it out rather than a vet having to get it out." I peered over at Declan. "I hope he doesn't get sick while I'm gone."

"He'll be grand." Declan didn't *sound* grand, still upset about my Andy comparison. "I'll go let him in." He headed toward the house where Mac was barking.

"Everything all right?" Zoe asked.

I shrugged.

"Not sure which is more difficult," she said, "having a fella or not having one. Had a brutal date last night."

My eyes widened. "Do tell."

Zoe hadn't dated anyone since I'd moved to Ireland.

She rolled her eyes. "His childminder canceled. He showed up with an eight-year-old son. Hadn't a clue he even had a kid. Rather than going for a lovely wine and steak dinner, we went to Eddie Rockets for burgers and shakes."

"They do have the best tater tots," I said, trying to lighten her mood.

She didn't laugh. "We were supposed to be going to that new horror flick, but I told him ya can't be taking a young lad to such a scary picture. He got pissed, telling me I shouldn't be judging his parenting. That I was no better than his ex-wife. When I told him he shouldn't be talking like that 'bout his ex in front of his son, he stormed out of the restaurant, leaving the little fella with me."

"Omigod. What'd you do?"

"Took him to a Disney picture until his mum got off work. Cost me forty-three euros for tickets and sweets. I ate three Cadbury bars."

"Sounds like you dodged a bullet. Was a good thing the guy brought his kid along, or you might have gone on a second or third date before learning he's a total jerk."

"If it hadn't been for that bloody arse, night wouldn't have been all bad. Was a good picture. The lad and I got on quite well. He asked me to his soccer game Saturday. Told him I had plans. Can't be going on a *second* date with an eight-year-old."

One more reason I needed to make things right between Declan and me. The thought of dating about made me break out in hives.

Gemma was driving to the meeting in County Kerry and supposedly had no room for me in her car, packed with meeting materials and suitcases. It was a three-day, fifty-person meeting. How much clothing and supplies did she need? She'd saved me from having to make up a lame excuse for taking the train.

During the three-and-a-half-hour train ride from Dublin, I kept forcing my gaze from sheep fields and my mind from the Andy argument with Declan. Things had been a bit awkward between us before I'd left. It was difficult to smooth things over when I was staying in a hotel several hundred miles away.

I needed to work on the Daly clan gathering, even though I should have time while manning the event's registration desk. It was crazy that Gemma couldn't handle a small meeting on her own. Yet she could do no wrong in the CEO's eyes. I was getting Flanagan's shit jobs, while she planned the glamorous ones.

Last month's executive glamping trip at the gypsy

caravans in County Galway had been such a success that I was planning another one in the fall. I should have prayed for a broken water pipe or a cow getting wedged between a caravan's stair railings, which both had happened on my site inspection with Zoe. I was also organizing the company picnic at Tayto Park. As much as I loved the potato chips, planning an amusement-park outing was far from glamorous or doing much to advance my career.

I focused on my computer, needing to figure out what to include in the *Daly Examiner*—a four-page pamphlet filled with fun facts about those attending the gathering. Daly clan bingo would include squares such as the oldest and youngest person there, the couple married the longest, and the person who'd traveled the farthest to get there. This event was way more fun to plan than your average meeting.

An e-mail from Fanny popped into my inbox, containing links for blue bridesmaid dresses with lots of chiffon and high collars. As if I was the grandmother of the bride. If I was dropping several hundred bucks on a dress, it had to be one I'd wear again and again. I had to find a dress pronto! Fanny also wondered if I thought it was proper etiquette to hold a shower for a second marriage. No! I didn't have time to plan a hen party and a shower. Yet wanting everything to be perfect for Fanny, I told her whatever she preferred was the appropriate thing to do. Screw Emily Post. I deleted my derogatory remark about the queen of proper etiquette and sent my reply.

My phone rang. Rachel. It was 3:00 a.m. in Milwaukee. *Sunnyvale* was blaring on the TV in the background. She'd been binge-watching the last few seasons to get up to speed on the storylines.

"I'm so psyched to hand in my notice today that I can't sleep. Aren't you excited?"

I took a calming breath. "Yeah, I'm excited for you but not for me. I'll likely be handling your meetings until they find a replacement."

The CEO would assume I'd be thrilled with a full-time position after my hours had been cut in March. My only big meeting was the September incentive trip to Dubrovnik, for which Rachel had helped me negotiate a killer contract, including concessions my company had never before received. I was a star planner. Yet I was planning the company picnic at Tayto Park.

"You should quit," Rachel said.

My sister hadn't wanted me to take the Flanagan's position, afraid I'd quit in a month if Declan and I broke up. That I didn't have staying power with anything in my life. Now she *wanted* me to quit?

"If it hadn't been for Flanagan's, I likely wouldn't be living in Ireland. I wouldn't have made the move without a security blanket and some financial stability. And my boss took a chance on me when nobody else would have with my lack of experience."

"You owe them nothing, same as I owe Brecker. They demoted you to part time and give you all the shit jobs, while ditzy Gemma stays at castles and stately homes. She's treated like a queen when she's really a jester, a total joke."

My grip tightened around the phone. This week's meeting at the Knockraven Manor House had been mine until my hours were cut. I'd been forced to hand it over to Gemma. However, I'd been ecstatic because it'd meant more time to focus on starting my genealogy business. Hmm...

"Most importantly, I need a steady income," I said.

"In three weeks, the estate will have plenty of work. I can hire you part time. Your loyalty should be to family, not Flanagan's."

This from a woman who'd missed half our family functions since starting with Brecker six years ago. Of course, I wanted the estate and Rachel to succeed. This past spring I'd been the one who'd gotten everyone on board with the art-mystery event to save the estate when George had been lying in the hospital with pneumonia. The estate's damp environment and financial upkeep had sucked the life out of our poor uncle. I couldn't leave Rachel high and dry even though she'd made the decision to become the estate's event planner.

"Hell, you can probably be full time," Rachel said.

"What if you don't get a ton of bookings for the events?"

"I'm sure we will."

"What if the show filmed an alternate ending and they don't get married? *Game of Thrones* filmed several endings for the series finale. A lot of series do. If *Sunnyvale* was so worried about it being leaked to the media that they didn't book the estate until two weeks before filming, they're taking precautions to make sure it remains a secret."

Silence filled the line.

I should have kept my yap shut. Yet Rachel had all these grandiose plans and needed to be prepared should the estate's episode not air.

"I can't believe you just said that," Rachel snapped. "Why would they spend all that money on the wedding episode if they aren't going to use it? You better not have just jinxed it."

So now it was *my* fault if Lawrence got ditched instead of hitched?

The train slowed, pulling up to the platform in Killarney.

"I'm sure you're right. Why would they spend all that money filming a bogus episode? Sorry I mentioned it. I gotta go. Will talk to you later."

I walked through the small station and encountered a poster with Caroline and Lawrence.

Will he be hitched or ditched?

"Hitched," a young woman said to her friend.

"She bloody well better not marry the arse."

"Betcha a pint she will. Better yet, make it a proper dinner at Donahue's."

My breathing quickened. I fought the urge to tear down the poster. Was there anyone who didn't watch the show? The estate was going to get slammed with events if...or rather *when* the couple got hitched. *Remain positive.* Rachel was right. Why would they have spent all that money on an episode they weren't going to use?

Yet I couldn't work four jobs!

My Flanagan's job was supposed to get me off the road and provide a steady income and stability, helping me find balance in my life. Right now I was feeling more unstable than ever!

I took a taxi to the luxurious stately home hotel. Upon entering the lobby, a refreshing minty scent relaxed the tension in my body. The place hosted weddings and special events, so I'd also be conducting corporate espionage for Rachel, checking out the competition. I snagged brochures from the front desk showcasing past events and detailing hotel amenities. The spa pamphlet mentioned their signature scent, rosemary mint. I inhaled the calming scent infused into the lobby.

According to the front desk, Gemma hadn't checked in. Big surprise. My room wasn't ready, so I swung back by the meeting space to get the lay of the land. As I was walking up to the room, Matthew McHugh, Flanagan's CEO, strode out with Henry Doyle, the company's head of security, and two of his staff. The security team left, and my boss joined me. Tall with salt-and-pepper hair, he was wearing jeans, a green tweed blazer, a white oxford shirt, and a green paisley print tie. He wasn't wearing his usual relaxed smile.

"Should I request Henry's team for the Dubrovnik incentive? I didn't realize they usually came on-site."

They hadn't for the glamping trip.

"No need. This being an integration meeting"—he glanced cautiously around—"we brought them on board." He apparently noticed my confused look and added, "Didn't Gemma mention the reason we needed another staff for the meeting is we just announced we're buying McHale's brewing company? We'll be eliminating some positions at the meeting today."

The first meeting I'd worked with Rachel in Dublin had taken place right after Brecker had bought Flanagan's. We'd been forbidden to even utter the word *integration*, even though no firing had occurred on-site.

The CEO walked away. I peeked inside the meeting room set with a hundred chairs. Gemma had also failed to mention this was now more than fifty people. I swapped out my flats for black heels and swiped on magenta lip gloss, which matched my dress.

An hour before the meeting started, my coworker strutted up in heels and a short green dress, full of lame excuses for her tardiness. It had probably taken her hours to put on her false eyelashes, black eyeliner, and three shades of eyeshadow, along with styling her long blond hair.

"Why didn't you tell me people are getting fired at this meeting?"

"It was confidential."

"I should have been prepared."

She rolled her blue eyes. "What? You wouldn't have come if you'd known?"

A growl vibrated at the back of my throat. I was ready to leap across the table and tackle her when the security team appeared. I smiled sweetly at them, placing name badges on the table.

Attendees began arriving just minutes before the meeting started. Nobody was anxious to receive their pink slips. One guy reeked of booze. He'd probably hit the minibar while still on the company expense account.

An hour into the meeting, a man in a suit raced from the room. He flew out the side door, Henry and another security guy hot on his heels. He hopped into a black Mercedes—likely a company car—and sped out of the parking lot. Henry was on the phone, to the garda, no doubt.

A guy snatched a basket of candy bars from the break buffet and dumped them into his briefcase.

"Those cost five euros each," Gemma said. "That's like five hundred euros in sweets." Her gaze darted to me. "Go stop him."

"I'm not stopping him."

I regretted not pocketing the bowl of gourmet mints on the human resources desk when I was fired from my first job out of college. I'd been a basket case thanks to my ex stalking me, but my employer hadn't been justified in firing me. My chest tightened, recalling the humiliation of the entire ordeal and the months of depression that followed. I swept a hand over my freshly shampooed hair, horrified at the thought of the greasy limp mess it had been when only washing it every few weeks.

A half hour later a guy bolted from the room, cradling his open laptop in the crook of his arm, typing frantically. Undoubtedly deleting confidential files or downloading them to a memory stick. Henry chased him toward the lobby.

Gemma popped up from her chair. "I have to go take a conference call."

"I'm not staying here alone with all these crazies."

"I have other meetings I'm working on."

"So do I."

"I'll be back in an hour." She strutted off.

I glared at her closed laptop on the table. Since when didn't you need access to your files for a client call?

I booted up my computer and tried to focus on the *Daly Examiner* to escape from the nuthouse.

My phone dinged. Declan texted a pic of Mac snoozing on Emily's green velvet couch, his legs in the air, not a care in the world. Oh, how I wished I were Mac. I smiled at the pic, glad that Declan wasn't too upset over our argument to not send me cute Mac shots. My dog would never go back to my apartment. Mac had lost his sense of purpose and direction since no longer herding sheep.

Had I also lost mine? Not focusing on my genealogy business?

Gemma returned an hour later, skin glowing, smelling like rosemary mint. She set a bag on the floor by her chair.

"What's that?"

"My lunch."

Liar! She'd be eating lunch off the meeting buffet same as me. I snatched a tube of rosemary mint lotion from the bag. The hotel's signature spa scent.

"I can't believe you were getting a spa treatment while I've been dealing with your meeting's bullshit."

I opened the top of the tube and swept it under my nose, inhaling the calming scent. Gemma grabbed for it. I yanked it away, my hand squeezing the bottle, a stream of lotion squirting into the air, landing on Matthew McHugh's silk tie as he exited the meeting room.

Gemma and I gasped.

He glared down at his designer tie, then over at me.

"Sorry," I muttered, my cheeks on fire.

The CEO tugged off his tie and thrust it at me. "Have this cleaned."

As if *I* was to blame for his damaged tie. I was, but ultimately it was Gemma's fault. Of course, he'd never blame his pet planner. I was not getting my second pink slip, especially because of this bitch. And I was not going back into a funk. I was leaving this job on my own terms.

"I quit," I blurted out, heart racing.

Panic filled Gemma's blue eyes. Her breathing quickened.

If I quit, she would be the new lead planner for the Dubrovnik incentive. In way over her head, our boss would finally realize how much she sucked.

The CEO shook his head in frustration. "I can't deal with this right now. We'll discuss it later."

Granted, this probably wasn't the best time to be handing in my notice, but I didn't like being brushed off as if my position was insignificant, like so many others at this meeting. Yet it gave me a chance to take back what I'd said. Maybe I'd quit in the heat of the moment thanks to my conversation with Rachel.

However, I felt a huge sense of relief over going from four to two jobs in a matter of minutes. Whereas Gemma was on the verge of hyperventilating, looking like she might pass out.

With all the *Sunnyvale* hype, the estate would be buried with bookings *when* the wedding episode aired. Rachel had just offered me a part-time job. More like she'd delegated it to me. Not being pulled in so many directions would help me focus on my genealogy business.

How I was going to start the business I had no clue.

But now I had no choice.

Despite having quit, I agreed to stay in Kerry and work the meeting. Gemma and I not speaking for two days was quite pleasant rather than awkward. After returning to Dublin, I'd gone into the office and briefed Gemma on my upcoming programs, including the Dubrovnik incentive trip. I'd been tempted to say, "Hope you find everything you need in my files." Precisely what she'd said three months ago when she'd given me a devious smile and last year's incentive trip binder to reference. The missing contracts and documents had made my job even more difficult. Being the bigger person, I'd kept the snarky comment to myself, which had probably made my coworker even more nervous.

Brecker had asked Rachel to stay on until her position was filled, but she'd said nope and given them two weeks' notice. She'd used the last of her frequent flyer miles to travel to England for the weekend and attend several wedding appointments with Fanny and me, including dress shopping. I was buying the first one that didn't make me look fifty years older.

Rachel was seated at George's antique library desk, filling in event dates on her Google calendar, preparing for an onslaught of *Sunnyvale* fans. "Hold those dates for the high-tea events. If we do three teas daily, we can take off Saturdays, unless of course we have a wedding booked. Offering individual reservations would be too difficult to manage. People might camp out here for hours, and we'd have to bounce them." She typed away, booking my schedule until I retired.

What happened to me being part time?

Organizing eighteen of the same tea parties weekly might sound like a no-brainer until a guest scalded her tongue on the hot tea and threatened to sue. Or another one swiped a prop from the film set and I had to tackle her as she made a getaway. Or Thomas flipped out when fans raided his flower beds to make souvenir bouquets. Just a few of the many things that could go wrong. Being an event planner had made me a diehard pessimist.

A cool breeze blew back the red drapes, carrying a floral scent from the garden. I wiped the sweat from my brow, trying to relax in the comfy tan upholstered chair. "Once I book clients at the clan gathering, I'll only be able to help part time."

Rachel nodded. An inspired look seized her face. "The clan gathering would make an awesome TV show. Like *Who Do You Think You Are?* I'm sure Robert Daly has connections. Maybe I should pitch it to him. What do you think?"

She'd gone stark-raving mad.

I eyed the framed wedding photo of Caroline and Lawrence on the cocktail table, and their engagement photo, which Rachel had pilfered from the show's website. Was that legal?

"If you're afraid of being slammed with events after the episode airs, should you keep coming up with more ideas?"

"We need to strike while the iron is hot. Another half dozen episodes they'll probably be divorced. Nobody will care about the wedding. And there *will* be a wedding."

Rachel was remaining optimistic despite my alternate-ending remark. That was so not like my sister.

"Have you watched the last few seasons?"

I shook my head. When did I have time to binge-watch a soap opera that aired five episodes weekly?

Her enthusiasm faded. "Please be a bit more excited about all the potential business. The estate is a financial wreck. There are two art-mystery events and a fall wedding on the books. That's it. We need some major business to get out of debt."

There was that "we" thing again. Granted, this was all my doing, but I hadn't thought I'd be helping *do* all these events. I didn't want to let George and Rachel down. I wanted to help make my sister's venture and the estate a huge success. Yet I also wanted my genealogy business to be one.

"You know what it costs to keep this place going? I just got the estimate for the new roof. I could buy a quaint cottage here for what it'll cost."

During the last rainstorm, the leak in my guest room had gone from a slow drip to gushing water taking hunks of plaster out of the ceiling. A grilling season of charcoal briquettes now filled the room. Keeping the moisture out of the house was a never-ending battle.

Rachel glanced over at the door. "I can't let George know about the roof. The stress of the estate's debt and upkeep will land him back in the hospital."

And my sister would be on dialysis when her bad kidney failed if she took on all the responsibility herself.

"If these events don't take off, I'm going to have to hunt down Diana and demand ten million pounds to not turn her in to the authorities."

In 1993 George's then wife had stolen valuable artwork from the Daly home, then ran off with the family's solicitor. The theft had started the estate's downward spiral to near bankruptcy.

I nodded. "I get it. And I'm going to help in any way I can. I just don't want to get in over my head. You agreed the clan gathering was a great way for me to get business. We included it as part of the package. I have to be able to take on clients."

Rachel nodded, grabbing the energy drink next to her computer. She was once again knocking back caffeine drinks after having quit that spring? Transitioning from Brecker to the estate job was supposed to reduce her stress.

"I thought you quit drinking those?"

She tapped a chipped red nail against the top of the can. The fact that her nails were a wreck and she had on jeans and a casual yellow top, rather than a designer dress, gave me hope.

"I did," she said. "I found this in the cupboard." She eyed the unopened can, then tossed it in the garbage.

"And I have George and Fanny's wedding on top of all this. The guest list is over a hundred. I'm happy for them, but the timing is horrible. Two weeks after the show airs, we'll be slammed."

"Hire a wedding planner." Someone who could also plan the hen party. Thankfully, Fanny had decided against the shower. Rachel needed to learn to delegate to people other than me.

"I'm not allowing some random planner to come in and take over. Not to mention, George couldn't afford to pay one." She glanced over at the door and lowered her voice. "He let Fanny believe we're making a ton off the *Sunnyvale* filming. It was good income, but we'll make a lot more from the events afterward."

"Are you going to be able to afford to hire a full-time planner if things take off?" What kind of crap pay was I going to be making? "I'm getting paid to help plan, right?"

She nodded. "Of course. After all the fanfare dies down in a few months, you can go down to part time. I'll just need you full time for the summer crunch. Would that work okay?"

I nodded. Between her desperate tone and pleading look, how could I say no? I needed the money and wanted to help, but I also knew my sister and her obsessive-compulsive tendencies. She'd continue sucking me into more and more events.

She smiled, a sparkle in her blue eyes. "Perfect. I really need you at the events since fans will want to hear firsthand from someone who attended the wedding."

Last fall when Rachel and I had worked together for

the first time, I'd been upset that she'd thought my dressing up as a sausage was the extent of my job skills. Suddenly, I'd kill for her to not have faith in me.

Fanny strolled into the room, a blissful look on her face, a box in her hand. "Since George is gone, I'll show you what I bought for the honeymoon." She slipped a slinky blue nightie from the box. "What do you think?"

Go Fanny.

Rachel smiled. "Gorgeous."

"Did the photographer confirm?" she asked.

Rachel nodded.

Fanny let out a relieved sigh. "Thank goodness."

The wedding photographer had taken Fanny's boudoir pics. One of her in a long blue dress and white fur stole, reclining on a pink settee, sat on a library shelf next to her historical romance novels. Would her new blue nightie be part of her wedding photo shoot?

"Can't wait for you young ladies to get married. It's like starting over. A whole new future on the horizon. I certainly hope you'll both be married here. Start a family tradition."

I didn't see marriage in my near future, the way things were going. Declan hadn't joined me last weekend in England for the first time ever. He'd claimed he wanted to stay home and finish Caroline and Lawrence's wedding portrait. Why couldn't he have painted it here? He always painted at the estate. He'd been happy that I'd quit Flanagan's so I could focus on my genealogy business. He wouldn't be thrilled when I told him I was also now a "temporary" full-time planner for George's estate.

"What do you think about having the London symphony perform at the wedding?" Fanny asked. "Not the entire symphony, of course, merely a few members. Like in that movie where the performers were seated among the guests and joined in one at a time with their instruments."

They'd have to sell the estate to afford it.

Rachel and I exchanged nervous glances.

"It's not in our budget, is it?" Fanny asked.

Since when did Fanny have a budget?

The woman's pale-blue eyes sharpened. "Is it?" Her stern tone threw us for a loop.

Rachel slowly shook her head.

"Neither is the lobster being shipped in from Maine?"

"How about lobster from a farm in Norway?" Rachel said.

Fanny dropped down on her blue velvet couch. "Darn that George. Why didn't he tell me that? I've looked like a fool thinking we made a windfall from that filming. Even if we had, I shouldn't have been wasting money on such nonsense."

"You were caught up in the moment," I said.

Rachel gave Fanny a sympathetic smile. "I'm sure I'll be the same way planning my wedding."

This was the first time I'd heard my sister voice marriage aspirations.

"We'll make loads off all the events after the show airs," Rachel said.

"Please don't tell George I know."

No problem. He wouldn't be happy we'd spilled the beans.

"He'll think I'm no better than Diana."

I gasped. "Don't you dare compare yourself to that nasty woman."

Yet I'd almost compared Declan to that bastard Andy. That was like George comparing Fanny to his ex-wife, Diana. Declan had every right to be ticked at me. He hadn't thought he was disrespecting me. He'd believed he was doing a good thing helping out Emily. I wished I could take back the comment.

"I'm not really keeping a secret from George," Fanny said. "It's a white lie to make him feel better. My marriage to Bernie would have been much better if I'd kept more secrets from him."

That was an interesting take on marriage.

"Not like Lawrence keeping his affair with that hussy a secret from Caroline before getting married."

The line between real and fictional characters was starting to blur for Fanny.

Whereas my *reality* was quickly becoming a blur.

Mac stood by my side, both of us staring out the bedroom window at the Coffeys' humble cottage down the hill. Hopefully, Grandma approved of me staying there while Declan was on a three-day work trip. After returning from England, I'd picked up Mac. He'd howled the entire way back to Dublin and then refused to get out of the car. Following an afternoon of dress shopping with Fanny and Rachel, I hadn't been in the mood for his attitude. At least the day had been a success. Fanny approved of a satin royal-blue bridesmaid dress that I could wear again, if I attended a ball at Buckingham Palace.

When I'd finally carried Mac from the car, whimpering, we'd gone upstairs to hear "You Are My Sunshine" on a ukulele and reruns of *Father Ted* blaring from another neighbor's place. Mac howled at each wrong chord. I explained to Mac we were going back to Emily's because the peace and quiet would allow me to focus on my genealogy business. Not because he'd won the battle. Having been against Declan moving to Emily's, I felt like a hypocrite staying there even though it was for our child's sake.

"Your great-grandma lived down there," I told Mac.

He pawed at the window cracked open enough to let fresh air in and prevent Mac from jumping out. Keeping Emily's windows open, and charcoal-filled foil pans in each room, had already helped reduce the musty smell. But even the sunshine couldn't perk up the navy walls. Fanny would turn up her nose at the dark, drab blue shade.

"No, you can't go visit. They no longer live there. A chicken lives there now, remember?"

A fly flew through the open window, and Mac chased after it.

"Hey, don't eat that. You never know what disease it might have." Not that eating a fly could be any worse than carrying that mouse around in his mouth a few months ago at George's. Thankfully, I hadn't encountered any mice here...yet.

I put my clothes away in an antique wooden dresser with a large mirror. I placed Grandma's framed photo on the dresser top's lace scarf. Taken in 1935 in front of Killybog church, the yellowed black-and-white photo was of Grandma and her sister Theresa, wearing bright smiles and mid-length dresses. Cloche hats and light-colored, shoulder-length wavy hair framed their faces. Grandma had noted on the back that her dress was pink, her hat cream with a pink silk rose. I'd also framed her and Michael's engagement photo. Grandma's silver brooch with emerald-colored stones was pinned to her high-collared lace gown. Michael had resembled a young Cary Grant, wearing a dark suit and a killer smile. A lump of emotion filled my throat at the thought of him having died two years later. It felt good defying his father's wishes by having the portrait of the forbidden engagement in the house.

I set a perfume bottle on the dresser top next to Declan's woodsy-scented cologne. The dresser scarf jerked, knocking over the bottles. Mac held the end of the scarf between his teeth and was tugging on it.

I clapped my hands. "Stop that!"

One vintage lace doily was still in the field between here and Grandma's house. Or at least Mac hadn't pooped it out. I certainly wasn't paying to have teeth holes mended in a dresser scarf.

Mac trotted off with a 'tude.

Not finding any damage to the scarf, I stashed it in a drawer. Hopefully, Emily wouldn't mind I was Mac-proofing her house. I couldn't afford to replace her needlepoint lace scarves and doilies, likely handmade by Irish nuns two hundred years ago in some poor convent, now worth thousands.

"I need to show you the alarm before Zoe gets here," Declan hollered up the stairs.

His sister was dropping him off at the train station so I could use his car while he was gone. I hadn't driven since my meltdown in England. I planned to sport the yellow reflective walking vest hanging on the coat rack downstairs.

I joined Declan at the alarm box by the front door.

"You press 09185 to set and unset the alarm." He pressed the numbers. *System arming.* It started beeping, warning us to vacate the house. "Unset it."

The warning beep continued.

My heart raced. "I don't remember the code."

Declan calmly repeated it.

I frantically typed it in. "I'll put the code in my phone."

"That's not safe. Ya need to be memorizing it. And take down Peter Molloy's mobile number."

"I'll be fine."

He gave me a stern look.

At least he was still worried about my well-being despite a bit of underlying tension between us.

"Fine." I input the number of his buddy, owner of Molloy's pub in Killybog.

"Sure you'll be okay here by yourself?"

"I was until you started freaking me out, acting like I *should* be worried." Major lie. Having never lived in the country, I was a bit nervous about staying here alone, even though I dreamed of living in rural Ireland. "I'll be too busy to be scared. Besides planning the clan gathering, I have my website to build and I'm attending a genealogy meeting." Nicholas Turney had invited me to the meetings numerous times. Sadly, I'd always been too busy to travel to the Midlands during the week.

I should have made the time.

Declan smiled that I would be dedicating time to my new business before becoming full time at the estate for a few months.

"Mac, take care of your mum while I'm gone. And Zoe is only twenty minutes away."

His parents' place had seemed like twenty *hours* from Molloy's pub when I'd had to drive Declan's drunk butt home last Christmas.

"I can always call Sadie or Seamus." Except my rellie Seamus didn't have a phone. And Seamus behind the wheel would be scarier than me behind one. Sadie wasn't allowed to drive due to some traffic violation she preferred not to discuss.

A horn honked outside.

Mac responded with a bark.

"Zoe. I gotta run."

We headed outside.

"Want to stop by later for a cocktail?" I asked Zoe. "You can crash here." Ireland's drunk-driving law was so strict even a glass of wine might put you over the legal alcohol limit.

She glanced in the rearview mirror at Declan tossing his suitcase in the trunk. "I have another date."

"I'm sure it'll go better."

Her gaze narrowed. "Could it be going any worse?"

I shook my head.

"I'll ring ya later," she said.

Declan gave Mac an affectionate rub behind the ears, then gave me a quick kiss. What was with the pathetic kiss? When saying good-bye, we usually shared a passionate one, as if he was going off to war rather than on a three-day work trip. What next? He'd be kissing Mac good-bye and rubbing me behind the ears?

Declan hopped into the car. I gave Zoe the *call me* gesture—thumb to my ear, pinky to my mouth. If Zoe had a boyfriend, we could double date. Fingers crossed her date went well.

At the end of the drive, Declan hopped out of the car and locked the gate. I watched them disappear down the road, recalling our depressing kiss. Making things right between us wasn't going to be easy, once again being apart.

Grandma's abandoned home was the only house in sight. In the distance, a neighbor's roof peeked over the top of some hedges. Rolling green fields with cows bordered Emily's Georgian-style stone house on both sides, and acres of woods occupied the land behind. Eight months ago I'd barricaded my Dublin hotel room door with furniture, despite having been surrounded by guests, hotel security just a scream away. I was no longer worried about Andy stalking me and felt safer here in the boonies than in the middle of Dublin. I was stronger and more self-sufficient now than before my relationship with Andy. That gave me a sense of pride and dignity. I had Declan to thank.

My phone dinged in my back pocket, startling me. An e-mail from Mom saying how much she loved my bridesmaid dress. Between Dad not being able to attend the wedding—having thrown his back out again—and her not having dress shopped with us, she sounded quite melancholy. If she wanted to be more involved with the wedding, how about planning the hen party?

Except my mom wasn't the best party planner. She'd organized my aunt Teri's husband's fiftieth birthday party. When she'd picked up his cake, she hadn't noticed that it'd read *Brain* instead of *Brian*. And an hour into the party, guests had blown through the snacks and there'd been a run on beer, something unheard of in Milwaukee—the beer capital.

I needed to learn to delegate like Rachel did to me.

Mom was now in charge of the hen party.

CHAPTER SEVEN

The next morning, I woke up on the edge of the bed facing the wall, Mac's paws pressing against my back. I turned toward my snoring dog sprawled across the mattress. I'd slept well, considering Mac was a total bed hog. I took a deep breath, inhaling Declan's woodsy cologne lingering on his pillow, which I slept on when he was away. My chest ached at the possibility of no longer waking up to the scent. I buried my nose in the pillow.

I snagged my phone off the nightstand and texted Zoe, asking how her date had gone last night. When she didn't respond, I slid off the bed and padded across the thin rug covering the wooden floor. I stripped off Declan's blue wool sweater I'd put on over my Coffey Dublin T-shirt during the night. I drew open the heavy drapes and blinked back the bright sunshine, a pleasant surprise following a night of rain. I smiled at Grandma's cottage below. Wanting to breathe fresh air into the room, I opened the window.

A loud *wrrring* pierced the silence.

The security alarm!

Mac sprang into action, howling, gaze darting around.

I raced down the stairs to the alarm box in the front hallway, Mac hot on my heels. Mac's howling and the alarm's beeping had me totally frazzled, unable to recall the deactivation code. I flew upstairs and grabbed my phone off the nightstand. Having ignored Declan's advice not to put the passcode in my phone, I located it as I ran back down to the box. I pressed in the numbers. The alarm stopped. My shoulders relaxed, but the ringing continued in my head. Mac kept howling.

"Mac, shut up!"

Surprisingly, he snapped his jaw shut, giving me the evil eye. As if I was the one being rude. I peeked out the front door. No neighbors or garda were rushing to my rescue. The gate was locked, but they could have been *running* up the drive. Across the field a farmer putzed along on his tractor.

The community watch program sucked.

I headed down the hallway past old man Daly's portrait smirking over my screwup. I grabbed a yellow floral tea towel from the kitchen and draped it over the painting. Emily promised no surprise visits. I'd uncover it before she stopped by.

I grabbed a sticky note from the desk in the peach room. I wrote down the passcode and slapped the paper on the alarm box. I'd have to remove it before Declan got home. He'd have a fit I hadn't memorized it.

On a tea and Tayto mission, I went into the kitchen, painted a horrible pea green with matching linoleum tiles. Painting the kitchen was a priority. If Declan didn't know how to tile a floor, he'd have to YouTube it. I nearly gagged at the thought of the mushy green veggie Mom added to half her dishes because Dad loved them.

I'd brought Taytos, peanut butter and jelly, deli meat, and all my favorite foods that required a microwave rather than Emily's humongous cast-iron stove, similar to George's. I flipped the switch on the electric kettle, and water soon started gurgling away. I'd brought a teacup from my Flannery family's china company in southern Wicklow. When Declan had been searching for Grandma's baptismal record in Arklow, the priest had passed his information along to a Susan Flannery. The widow ended up being related to me through marriage. Sadly, all my Flannerys had immigrated to Australia.

Mac dragged his bowl over and dropped it in front of me. I filled the stainless-steel dish and carried it, along with tea and Taytos, on a silver tray into the peach room. I set the tray on the cocktail table and moved an old photo album to the side so I didn't spill on it.

My phone dinged. A text from Zoe.

Don't even ask.

That bad?

I waited with nervous anticipation for her response.

When I showed him snaps of my pet apparel, he shared snaps of his pet iguana, Fergus. Wanted me to knit it a cap. The bloody beast was scary as hell. Looked like something from Jurassic Park. Would eat poor Quigley for breakfast. Told him I wasn't feeling well and left. Was true. Thought I was going to puke at the sight of the yoke. Will be having nightmares for weeks...

I replied with a frowning face emoji.

The possibility of double dating wasn't looking promising.

I checked e-mail to find three new registrants for the clan gathering. Yay! A total of sixty-seven. Fanny had e-mailed Rachel and me wondering about selling tickets for her wedding to *Sunnyvale* fans to help cover her expenditures. Rachel had responded that her wedding should be personal and intimate. They'd earn money from other events. Before Gerry and her new job, Rachel would have been all about the money.

I slammed my cup of tea while reading my sister's e-mail with her latest idea to have actors from Dalwick's local theater group play the roles of Caroline and Lawrence at the tea events. Attendees would receive wedding favors, as if actual wedding guests. Rachel had attached dozens of ideas for favor souvenirs on Pinterest. The soap opera had approved use of the promo wedding shot on items sold at the estate, but not online. She'd had great foresight when she'd contracted the concessions that would come in handy with upcoming *Sunnyvale* events. Yet I couldn't even get a break from *Sunnyvale* hell when she was over the middle of the Atlantic!

My breathing quickened at the thought of my pruned fingers washing five loads of fine china by hand daily. Scrubbing marmalade and clotted cream stains from the library's oriental rug. Polishing the silver. Sweeping up mouse droppings...

Caityrella, Caityrella!

Would Rachel become my wicked stepsister?

The overhead light flickered off, and I lost my internet connection. Lovely. Either the electricity was out or a fuse was blown. Did they have fuses in Ireland? Hopefully, that's all it was, so I didn't have to call the electric company. Understanding the Irish accent over the phone wasn't easy.

A loud knock sounded at the front door.

Heart racing, I dropped to the floor on all fours.

It was awfully coincidental that someone was knocking on the door right after the electricity went out. The electric company certainly hadn't made it here that quickly.

Another knock.

My heart pounded.

Rather than remaining safely hidden like me, Mac barked, racing to the front door to greet our visitor. He was much too trusting. Maybe it was the postman with a package too big for the mailbox on the stone fence by the gate. I wasn't going to answer the door in my jammies. I didn't have a bra on under my green Coffey Dublin T-shirt, and my plaid leggings were skintight.

I crawled over to the window and peeked out at a tall guy—thirtyish, dark hair, cute. Mac ran up and stuck his nose against the glass, barking. The guy's startled gaze darted to Mac and me on all fours peering out at him. He approached the window with a curious look.

"Hello there," he said with an American accent, yelling through the glass.

I slid the window up a crack and stood.

"My name's Liam. I attend Trinity College in Dublin. Wondering if it'd be okay if I take a look at the house in the woods back behind here."

A fly flew in the window, and Mac was off in hot pursuit.

Great guard dog.

"I don't know of any house in the woods. But I just moved in, so not sure."

"I was told it's on the Dalys' property."

"There is a slew of Dalys in the area."

"This was the location I was given." He held up a hand-drawn map scribbled on a piece of paper. It could have been a map of any road and house, or his three-year-old's art project. "It was an IRA hideout."

The hairs on my arms shot up. My limited knowledge of the IRA came from the movie in which Brad Pitt's attempt at a Belfast accent made me cringe.

The guy apparently realized I was a tad freaked out and gave me a reassuring smile. "It's for my thesis paper."

"Let me call the owner." Or the garda.

This gave me a weird vibe. However, Emily's creepy grandfather would roll over in his grave if the Irish Republican Army, whose goal was to overthrow English rule, had once had a hideout behind his house. Talk about karma.

"I need to go upstairs for a better signal and to wake up my husband." I didn't want him to think I was here alone.

I also wasn't calling Emily. No way was I staying in the house alone while a stranger skulked around in the back woods searching for an IRA house. I headed upstairs and returned a few minutes later.

"She didn't answer. You could check with the postmaster, or there's a group of old men who hang out at Molloy's pub in Killybog. I'm sure they'd be familiar with it."

"Would you mind if I just take a look?"

I minded very much, though I felt bad that he needed this info to finish his thesis. Also, I wasn't sure how Emily would feel about me allowing him on her property. She was a very private person. Declan would wig out that I was even considering it.

"Give me your number. I'll contact the owner and let you know on the house." He could come back next week when Declan was here.

The disheartened-looking guy gave me his number. I loaded it in my phone. He hiked down to the end of the drive and climbed over the gate. He motored off in a tiny gray car, grinding gears filling the quiet morning. Likely a rental, since you wouldn't need a car living in Dublin. Car rental companies charged an insane price for automatic vehicles, yet their insurance didn't cover transmissions. What a racket.

I slipped on my purple wellies by the coatrack. I walked outside for cell service to call Declan about the electrical outage and inquire on how to replace a fuse. I headed down the tree-lined dirt drive, avoiding puddles from last night's rain. I opened the gate, not wanting to appear antisocial. Especially since my Dublin neighbors now thought I was a raging lunatic. Two bars popped up on my phone. Rather than FaceTiming Declan, I called. After that pathetic good-bye kiss, I needed to step up my game. At least comb my hair and whisk on some mascara before he saw me.

"Ah, shite, forgot the electric is being shut down from nine to three for a new installation in the area."

"So they cut off *everyone's* service when someone gets a new installation? What about stuff in the freezer and fridge?"

"Open them as little as possible to keep things cold. At least it's not the dead of winter, or you'd be without heat and have to be keeping a fire lit."

"Worse than no heat, I have no internet. I have to finalize a bazillion things for the clan gathering this weekend and work on my genealogy website. If I don't get stuff to the printer before Thursday, who knows if it'll be done in time."

Yet, no internet meant no e-mails from Rachel. Hmm...

"The library in town likely has internet."

"At least it's only a mile away." I could walk it.

"Doubt Killybog has a library. I meant Dunmoor."

"Where's that?"

"Two miles west."

I'd have to drive for the first time since England.

"Gotta run. Will ring ya later."

Click.

No "I love you"? We never hung up without saying "I love you."

Something was definitely off between us.

I also hadn't had a chance to mention the IRA guy. Probably better I didn't tell Declan. No sense in both of us being freaked out over it. And I didn't want to play the damsel in distress. When I'd worked as a travel staff, Declan had constantly saved my butt and had my back. I wanted to prove to him I could take care of myself while staying here.

A loud squawking filled the air.

Speaking of being self-sufficient...

I went over to Grandma's cottage and peeked in the window. My visitor was once again perched on the brick Declan had replaced in front of the door. He'd insisted if the door remained open, every stray animal would live there. I didn't think that was a bad thing. Yet besides the animals damaging the home, he also feared that the harsh winds and rain would strip off the remnants of paint and cause the plastered stone walls to crumble.

The hen let out another squawk, sounding like a cantankerous old woman.

"If you can fly in the window, you can fly out it."

The bird glared at me, then at the door.

"Come here. I'll help you." I gave it an encouraging smile. "You can do it."

The chicken's squawking grew louder, clipped with a hint of annoyance.

Fine. I was just trying to help.

I slowly pushed open the door.

The bird waddled out and over to the open gate without a thank-you.

"Ungrateful bird," I called after it.

I couldn't train my own dog. How did I think I was going to train some rogue chicken?

CHAPTER EIGHT

Since I couldn't shower, work, or even make tea, I threw on jeans, a white T-shirt, and tennies and tossed my hair up in a clip. Emily's valuables were stashed away, so I agreed not to put Mac in a kennel while I was gone, as long as he behaved. The kennel was an empty threat since I didn't own one, but Mac didn't know that. He fell asleep on the bed, and I headed downstairs, giving myself a pep talk. Driving on these narrow one-lane roads with huge tractors, old men walking dogs, and escaped sheep would be a breeze compared to England's eight-lane highway I'd had a meltdown on.

I flew out the front door and nearly slammed into my elderly cousins Sadie and Seamus, along with a woman they introduced as their friend Imelda. A brown tweed suit swallowed Seamus's thin frame, and the women wore dresses. They always looked like they were off to church.

"Didn't think ya were home. Been ringing the bell." Seamus squinted past me into the house. His thick black-framed glasses weighed heavy on his hollow cheeks.

"Sorry. Electricity is out."

My cousin Sadie—petite with tightly curled gray hair—held an apple tart. My stomach growled despite having eaten two bags of Taytos and one of Fanny's scones.

"Just calling in with a few housewarming gifts," she said.

Seamus held up a small box. "Teacups from our great-granny's collection."

"How wonderful. But I haven't actually moved in here. Just staying a few days while Declan is away for work."

They nodded faintly, as if unsure about my living arrangements.

"I hope it doesn't bother you that I'm staying here at the Daly house."

Sadie wore a baffled expression. "Why ever would it, luv?"

Of course, I was the only one bothered by it.

They craned their necks to see around me.

I needed to get to the library for internet access. My website had to be completed before the genealogy meeting tomorrow so I could ask experts' opinions on it. However, I regretted not having ever attended a genealogy meeting with Nicholas. I'd certainly regret not taking time to have tea with Seamus and Sadie. The library would have to wait. I'd worked hard to find Grandma's niece and nephew. I wasn't going to alienate them on their first visit. And Sadie's tart smelled delish.

"I'm sorry. Come inside."

They stepped into the foyer, peering curiously around and down the hallway.

"Looks 'bout how I'd expected," Seamus said.

Imelda nodded. "Yeah, dark and eerie."

Sadie shot her a disapproving glance.

"What's the Daly woman like?" Imelda asked. "She was ten years my senior."

Spending little time here, Emily was a bit of a mystery to her neighbors. When I'd visited Sadie and Seamus on the other side of Killybog last Christmas, they hadn't a clue who lived here, merely rumors of a woman from Dublin. Wanting to debunk local gossip that Emily was a scary old witch, I now told them all kinds of great things about her.

"So you grew up just down the road?" I asked Imelda.

She nodded. "Still live in the family home."

"Have you ever heard of a house in the woods behind here?"

"The old IRA hideout?"

I nodded, a chill slithering up my back.

"Mightn't still be there. May have crumbled to the ground by now. Me brother Sean and his mates would spend Halloween night there. Or rather they tried, but they always got the pants scared off them halfway through the night and would come racing home."

Sadie and Imelda exchanged mysterious looks, as if the place was haunted. I had a chicken in Grandma's house—I better not have a ghost in this one or the one out back.

The hairs on my arms stood at attention.

"I accidentally triggered the alarm this morning. Did you hear it?"

Imelda shrugged. "Might have. The alarm here was always sounding, so nobody thinks anything of it anymore. The security company eventually turns it off. Johnny Neil used to check on the place, but nobody was ever breaking in. Should I hear the alarm, I'll certainly be checking in now that I know you're staying here."

"How 'bout that tart?" Seamus said impatiently.

We sat at a weathered table in the backyard, eating apple tart and drinking water, since I couldn't offer tea. I opened my gift. Three teacups from my great-grandma Mary Flannery Coffey's collection. My favorite had a quaint stone bridge with green hills in the background.

"These are lovely."

"Quite excited for Fanny's hen party," Sadie said. "Never been to one. Wasn't done at the time we were married."

I needed to get hold of Fanny's guest list for this party. How many had she invited? Granted, Sadie and George were related, but the two women had never even met.

"Me daughter Peggy had one," Imelda said. "Saw male dancers down in Cork. I couldn't make it on account of a nasty flu. Sounded like great craic."

Not sure if Emily or Mom would approve of a strip club. However, I could see Fanny and my aunt Dottie showing up with wads of dollar bills.

"What would you think of a dinner cruise on the Liffey?" I said. The next best thing to one on the Seine.

Sadie's nose scrunched with disapproval. "Might be a bit tame for a hen party."

"Unless the boat has strippers," Imelda said.

"Me granddaughter did one of them CSI yokes,"

Seamus said. "Had to find the missing groom before the wedding."

"Was he naked when they found him?" Imelda asked.

Seamus gave the woman a disgusted look and shoved a forkful of tart into his mouth.

That CSI event was a great idea, without the naked groom. I'd pass it along to Mom.

"Speaking of weddings," Imelda said. "Might ya care to buy a raffle ticket for the church fundraiser?" She removed a stapled packet of tickets from her purse. "You choose if he'll be hitched or ditched. The winner will be selected from tickets with the correct answer."

My breathing quickened. Even in rural Ireland I couldn't escape the *Sunnyvale* hype and fear of being an event planner for life!

"Prizes include a router, hedge trimmer, and a fifty-euro Tesco voucher."

Seamus shook his head. "Would rather be putting a few extra quid in the basket at Sunday Mass than paying ten euros for one of them tickets. Can't believe ya be watching such nonsense."

"Been watching it since the first episode in 1972," Sadie said with a firm nod.

The soap opera had been around twice as long as I had. No wonder the fans spanned generations.

"Me too," Imelda chimed in. "Caroline was born 'bout the same time as me granddaughter Anya. And they attended Trinity together."

Sadie smiled. "Ah, right, that was a lovely graduation."

Caroline's or Anya's?

Fanny wasn't the only one who had a hard time drawing the line between reality and *Sunnyvale*.

"I'll take five tickets," I said.

With any luck, they'd remember my generosity when they learned they hadn't been invited to the wedding's filming. And I hoped I didn't win the router because I hadn't a clue what it was.

Two pieces of tart and an hour later, I was standing out front saying good-bye to my guests when a small white car puttered up the driveway.

"Militant Mattie," Sadie said. "Don't be letting him bully ya." A quick hug and they were off, car doors slamming shut before Mattie opened his. They gave him a faint wave.

The short, gray-haired man wore tan cotton pants and a blue polo shirt. "So glad I caught ya and that someone is finally living here. I'm Mattie McGuire. On the Killybog Tidy Town committee."

I shook his hand. "Caity Shaw."

"Ah, a Yank, are ya?"

I nodded, smiling. Even though I'd never been called a *Yank* in a derogatory manner, I'd rather be referred to as a *blow-in from America*. It was how the locals referred to Irish from another county. *Ah, a blow-in from Tipperary, are ya?* As if Tipperary were another country rather than a county ten miles from the Westmeath border.

"Being you're new to the area, I wanted to get ya up to speed. Killybog is in the running for Tidy Town this year. Your house being at the village limits is visitors' first perception. Approach roads are just as important as village streets. Worth fifty marks. I'm not the only one who believes this place has kept us from winning in past years. I'm sure ya won't be wanting to let down your new neighbors." He handed me a schedule for *Roadside Rubbish Duty*, with today's date circled.

What about letting down my family when I got picked *off* while picking *up* litter on these narrow roads? I was all for the Tidy Town cause. Besides the friendly Irish people, the country's quaint villages and towns were a major tourist draw. But was I willing to risk my life for a tidy community?

"The landscaping is quite the eyesore, isn't it now?" He gestured toward the dead bushes along the front of the house and then the gate at the end of the drive. "And that could certainly benefit from a coat of paint. Judging takes place over the summer, so time is of the essence. The winner is announced in September." He scurried back toward his car. "I'm off to Flaherty's. They haven't been helping our marks none either."

He puttered back down the drive. He'd likely be back soon to check on our landscaping progress. I didn't have time today to pick up garbage. Declan would have to address the man's concerns when he returned.

He'd wanted to be the caretaker of Emily's place, and according to Mattie, it needed a lot of care.

⚜ ⚜

On the drive to the library, I encountered a Guinness truck barreling down the narrow road. God forbid a pub had a run on beer, but no worries if someone was run off the road into a field. I swerved over to the shoulder, sideswiping a row of hedges likely camouflaging a stone fence. Upon arriving in Dunmoor—a village of around a thousand residents—I parked on the town square. I peeled my fingers from the steering wheel. At least I'd made it there unharmed—physically anyway—and an hour before closing. According to the sign, they were only open three days a week.

Before heading inside, I checked my e-mail, taking advantage of having three bars on my phone. One from Rachel included more links to wedding favors on Pinterest. I replied, explaining Emily's electrical outage and my sketchy cell service. I promised to be in touch when the internet was back up, not mentioning that would be in just a few hours.

The library shared a building with a Chinese takeaway restaurant. When I entered, the scent of sweet-and-sour sauce filled the air. Kung Pao Chicken sounded great for dinner. I smiled at the Asian woman on the phone taking an order. A side door with a glass window led into the library. Besides the librarian, the only person there was the IRA guy seated at a table. He glanced up from a book and smiled—a friendly welcome considering I was preventing him from completing his thesis.

"The men weren't in the pub, and the postman wasn't sure about the house's location. Thought I'd see if I can find anything in the local history section here."

His persistence gave him some legitimacy. I nodded, feeling bad and a bit guilty since I now knew the truth. "After you left, I was talking with a neighbor who said that house is behind where I'm staying. Or at least it was thirty years ago."

His face lit up. "Would it be okay if I take a look for it?"

"Ah, sure."

Would Emily mind if I let someone traipse across her land without me being there? I could lock myself in the house. Except I had no electricity to activate the alarm. However, this guy wasn't giving me a weird vibe like when I was alone in the boonies without electricity, a security alarm, phone service... Actually, I was curious to see what an IRA hideout had looked like. I knew little about the conflict, and this guy appeared to be a wealth of information. I wasn't going to get much done here with only an hour of internet service. I'd be better off at Emily's and starting work at three when the electricity came back on, working into the night.

Justification at its finest.

"I'll go with you."

Upon reaching our cars, I let out a frustrated groan at a slew of scratches on my passenger door. I was going to hunt down that Guinness truck driver and make him repair it. Part of me being self-sufficient was not having Declan privy to all my mishaps.

"I have something that will make that look good as new," Liam said. He grabbed a plastic bottle from his car and handed it to me. "Most petrol stations sell buffing cream that will take those scratches right out."

Good tip. "Thanks."

"Consider it a thank-you for helping me out."

The drive to Emily's wasn't as traumatic as the trip to the library. My confidence was bolstered by a large tractor clearing the road of oncoming traffic. For once I wasn't the one pulling over to the side, allowing others to pass. It was usually a game of chicken, and I was always the loser.

When we arrived at Emily's, Mac was at the window, barking. No way was he tagging along and running off in the woods. I was afraid to leave him unattended in the fenced-in backyard for fear he'd tunnel his way out. He was quite motivated, except when it came to being trained.

At the edge of the woods, a narrow clearing now overgrown with shrubs and grass was likely once the drive to the IRA hideout. We followed it back a half mile to a two-story stone house with a moss-covered roof. Ivy trailed up the side of the house and through the glassless windows. The roof on the stone out-building had caved in, and a tree was growing up inside it.

I could see where the haunted stories had come from.

A light mist filled the air, giving the place an even eerier feel. A shiver crawled up my back.

Liam came to a halt, staring at the house, then over at me. "You've been so nice that I need to tell you the truth."

The truth? My heart raced. What perfect timing for telling me the truth, alone in the middle of the woods. What had I been thinking, going with a stranger into the woods without telling anyone? Declan would kill me.

If this guy didn't first!

"I'm not actually writing a thesis."

I took a cautious step back, preparing to bolt.

He shook his head. "Sorry. I don't mean to scare

you. I really am attending Trinity, but I'm not writing a thesis. The truth is my parents met in this house. They were members of the IRA. My mom was pregnant when my dad was killed in a bombing. She moved to the US and never talked about him until recently. After a lot of convincing, she drew me the map for this place."

What a horrific, yet kind of romantic, story. I could relate to wanting to find the family homestead.

"My dad's last name was likely McCarthy, Gregory, or Flood."

"She wasn't sure who your father was?" I snapped my mouth shut. "Sorry. That's none of my business."

He let out a faint laugh, easing the tension in the air. "No, she knew who he was—just refused to share his name. Didn't want me contacting his family. They'd had a falling out. I researched IRA bombings within the nine months prior to my birth, and those men were killed—1985 was filled with a lot of unrest."

"I understand about closure."

I shared my journey to finding my Coffey home, recalling the first time I'd visited it with Sadie and Seamus. Imagining how Grandma had felt when walking out the yard's rusted gate for the last time. How emotional I'd become standing on Coffey ground and later discovering Grandma's heartbreaking past.

"What an inspirational story," Liam said. "Gives me hope. Maybe I could hire you to find out who my father was. I've gotten nowhere with DNA tests."

Hmm... My story *was* inspirational. I should share it on my website. Not only would it add to my research experience but it would demonstrate my passion for genealogy. My perseverance to not stop until I found answers. I was my fourth client. And Liam was my first prospective one in months. Yet I was leery taking him on with the clan gathering that weekend. And if DNA couldn't connect him with rellies, I wasn't sure I could.

"I'm not taking on new clients, but maybe I can refer you to someone." A member at the genealogy meeting tomorrow might be able to help him out.

Liam walked up to the house and placed a hand gently on the rough stone exterior.

"You should take a stone. I have one from my Coffey home."

He smiled, wiggling one free. He squeezed it in his hand, closing his eyes, as if hoping to channel his father.

If only stones could talk...

Despite the spitting rain, we explored the house, looking for signs of his parents. But their names weren't carved into a wooden beam, and no pics of them were left behind. The house was empty except for rusted beer cans and lots of sheep poop. We returned to Emily's, and the sky cleared.

"I can't thank you enough. This was an incredible experience." Liam's eyes watered, staring at the stone in his hand. "To actually have a piece of the home where my parents met. Even though it wasn't under the best circumstances or a traditional family home, it means a lot to me."

I swallowed the lump of emotion in my throat, glad I'd agreed to help him. That I'd been a part of his journey. Especially if he never learned his father's identity. I needed to help people find their ancestors' homes. To provide them with a physical, not only an emotional, connection to their Irish heritage.

After Liam left, I brushed wet hair from my face and stared into the woods, still a bit freaked out that the IRA had hid out here, formulating their revolutionary plans. The Dalys couldn't have known what was going on or they'd never have allowed it. Had anyone even lived in Emily's house in the 1980s? I was anxious to tell her about my visitor. Hopefully, she was okay with me having let him take a look.

I headed inside, into the peach room.

I came to an abrupt halt. A furry creature the size of a squirrel with a pointed snout was snoozing on the green velvet couch next to Mac, their heads resting on a lace pillow.

The overhead light and lamps flashed on.

I let out a startled scream.

Mac sprang up. The critter flew from the couch and slipped out the partially open window he'd likely entered through.

Problem solved. For now.

Just one more reason besides flies that Ireland needed screens on their windows. I couldn't keep the house closed up. It was just starting to smell better.

Mac was racing around the room, trying to figure out what had caused my scream.

Heart still pounding, I shook my head. "You definitely aren't K-9 material."

I sat at the desk, peering down at the Coffey cottage, psyched to share my ancestry journey on my website. And to add my service of locating family homes. It would be interesting to interview neighbors to learn a home's history. Like Imelda's story about her brother and friends attempting to spend Halloween in the hideout. However, I'd better wait until tomorrow's meeting and inquire on the availability of land records needed to find the homes. I hoped the genealogy club's members were as welcoming and supportive as Nicholas had been.

I had to start and *finish* my website before going to bed. I wasn't tech savvy, but Rachel had turned me onto a user-friendly site she'd ended up using for the estate, not wanting to rely on Brecker's web designer to update one. A good thing since she'd no longer have access to the company's employee.

I typed in the website builder's address.

No internet connection.

Seriously? The electricity was on, but the modem box in the window had a weak signal. I moved it to a window on the other side of the room. No signal. The home's walls were twice as thick as a modern home. I opened a window to see if the glass made a difference. I set the box too close to the edge, and it fell out onto the ground. The green lights lit up. A full signal. Luckily, it no longer looked like rain.

This was one instance where it was a good thing Ireland homes didn't have screens on their windows.

"Where are you?" I asked the mechanic on the other end of the phone. "I said to go south and take a right at the crossroads and then a left. I'm the fourth or fifth house on the right."

I was trying to be patient since this guy was making a house call at a moment's notice. But I was going to be late for my genealogy meeting. He was more directionally challenged than I was. Emily didn't have a house or a fire number. The address on her mail merely read Killybog, Mullingar, County Westmeath.

"I'm on the Kinbar road heading toward Glenteen."

Declan's parents lived in Glenteen twenty minutes from here. My grip tightened on the phone.

"Go back to Killybog. I am literally one kilometer from town. Face the sun and turn right. That's my road."

"Would be much easier if ya had yer Eircode."

I apologized again for not knowing Emily's Eircode. And Declan and Emily weren't answering my calls. If I had one in Dublin, I had no clue what it was.

He guaranteed me he'd be there in fifteen minutes and disconnected. This was a good dry run should I ever have an emergency. I needed to know the Eircode, or Mac and I'd be dead before anyone found us.

I wasn't merely cranky over possibly missing my first genealogy meeting and having been up until 2:00 a.m. working on my website. I was worried I'd done damage to Declan's car. It'd made a horrible noise when I'd tried to shift without having the clutch in. Now it didn't start. With my luck, it was probably something expensive like the transmission.

I was proud of myself for calling a mechanic rather than Declan for help, my first instinct. I was proving I could stand on my own here in the middle of nowhere. Getting a critter out of the house. Fixing the internet service and Declan's car. Staying in a huge house by myself without electricity.

Yet I wished Declan were here with me.

My phone rang. Emily. I'd hoped it was Declan. We hadn't spoken since yesterday morning when the electricity had gone out. He hadn't answered my call last night. However, he'd texted, reminding me to set the alarm. Which had also reminded me to remove the sticky note with the alarm's code before he returned. I assured myself that his lack of contact was because he was busy, not because he no longer cared.

I explained to Emily that I'd been trying to reach her for the Eircode. She gave me the code, and I typed it into my phone.

"An American guy was here yesterday looking for the old house in the woods. I hope it's okay I let him go back."

"People come looking for it now and then. Historians and such. Rather a nuisance. It's none of their business what went on there."

Crap. I shouldn't have allowed Liam on her land.

"Actually, Liam's parents lived there in the eighties. His father was killed. He never knew him. Felt bad for him."

Silence filled the line.

"Are you there?" I asked.

"Yes...I am."

"He'd researched bombings in 1985, trying to discover his father's identity."

"His father was killed in a bombing?" she muttered.

"Yeah, so sad." Maybe the tragic story would make her compassionate about Liam's visit. "Did you ever happen to hear the names of the members in the hideout?"

"I must go, dear," she said with a clipped tone.

Click.

Lovely. If Emily was upset enough to kick us out, Declan would claim I'd done it on purpose.

I was using Liam's cream and a soft cloth to buff the scratches from Declan's car door when Zoe texted.

Walked into the restaurant last night and only one fella sitting alone. A candle on the table started his menu on fire. He tried to blow it out, and the flame torched his paper napkin. Rather than helping the bloke, I burst into tears and left. Had a bloody breakdown.

My shoulders slumped. *Sorry third time wasn't a charm.*

Poor Zoe. Too bad I didn't know any nice guys in Ireland I could set her up with.

The mechanic drove up in a small blue truck.

A few minutes of looking under the hood, and he said, "Wire damage. Probably field mice."

"A stray animal was in the house yesterday. It looked kind of like a squirrel. Wonder if that was it."

"Pine marten. Type of weasel, it is. My aunt had one in her house a few weeks ago. Not sure what they're up to lately. But this was likely a mouse." He held up a ratty-looking wire. "Good news is it's minor damage. I've come across much worse."

"Do you have any of those wires on you?"

A loud squawking carried up the hill from Grandma's.

For the love of God.

"Just so happens I have some in my lorry. This is a fairly common occurrence."

How common of an occurrence? As common as flies in Emily's house or a chicken in Grandma's?

While the mechanic replaced the wire, I went down and opened the cottage's door. "I don't have time for pep talks so just get on your way."

The bird waddled past me, beak in the air.

"What did you do before I was staying here?"

It probably flew out the window and went home.

Like driving in Ireland, was this another game of chicken in which I always gave in first?

Not anymore.

I entered Carter's pub. The owner, Mags, waved from behind the bar, calming my nerves about meeting everyone. In her early forties, she was petite with brown hair and a no-nonsense attitude that could clear the pub at closing time. Mac trotted over for a few of his favorite treats. He gobbled them up, then lay down next to the unlit fireplace. Mags had my dog better trained than I did.

The genealogy meeting was already in progress. A group of five men and women sat at the chairs and tables to the side of the bar. I was at least thirty years younger than any member. No surprise, since the meetings were held on a weekday. Everyone's gazes darted to me. A thin, gray-haired man in navy slacks and a white dress shirt gave me a kind smile. His wooden cane rested against the table. The cane resembled Nicholas's—a knotty pine with a crack at the top. I recognized the man from Nicholas's wake. My first wake had been a bit traumatic, seeing my elderly friend laid out on his living room couch, his pet rabbit, Stewey, sleeping on his chest. Declan and I'd left after a few minutes.

"So sorry I'm late." I pulled up a chair, introducing myself. Everyone seemed to recognize my name, as if Nicholas had spoken of me. "A mouse chewed through a wire in my car, and I had to have it fixed."

A man in jeans, an orange T-shirt, and a neon-yellow walking vest nodded. "Aye, one of them rascals once stuffed loads of dog kibble in me air filter. Can do a fair amount of damage, they can."

"Me sister placed a stuffed owl next to her car," said a lady pushing up an oversized pair of red glasses on her nose. "The rodents don't be liking the bird."

"Fresh mint under the hood does the trick," said a

lady with a tightly curled black wig that made her look even paler.

"What about mint tea?" A plump lady snagged two biscuits from a plate and stashed them in her purse.

"As if ya be needing to show a wee bit of hospitality before getting rid of the yoke?" the wig lady asked.

The man with the cane got the group back on track. He introduced himself as Mickey and said he'd been a history professor, same as Nicholas. Two members held master's degrees in genealogy. One was a librarian, and another worked in the archives at the National Library in Dublin. They all had one thing in common: genealogy was either a part-time or retirement gig for them.

When I told them I was an event planner, everyone raised curious brows. I explained the Daly clan gathering I was organizing.

"Ah, brilliant," the wig lady said. "Will give ya access to potential clients as well as an income from steady work."

"I've only had three clients. I'd appreciate any advice."

"Well, luv, ya should be joining the Genealogical Society of Ireland," the biscuit hoarder said.

The wig lady nodded. "My yes, wonderful for networking. They meet once a month just south of Dublin. I've attended several lectures. Quite good, they are. Their volunteer projects would help ya gain experience. The Irish Genealogical Research Society would also be a good one to join."

I scribbled the info down on my notepad.

"My friend teaches a ten-week intensive course in Dublin on Irish records and research methods," Mickey said. "You receive a certification—Diploma in Family History. Other courses can eventually lead to a proper degree in family history and genealogy."

"You're lucky to be in Dublin with access to so many opportunities," said glasses lady.

I nodded but didn't feel lucky, since Declan was in Killybog.

The yellow-vest guy massaged his stubbly chin. "Being a Yank, ya should reach out to Irish organizations in America, get your name out there."

"I'm also trying to get my name out there with a website. I'd love to get your guys' opinions, if you don't mind."

"That's what we be here for, luv," Mickey said.

I booted up my laptop. What I lacked in experience I'd made up for with flair, wowing website viewers with scenic pictures of Ireland. Grandma's pic with her sister and one of her family's cottage highlighted my Coffey journey, which intrigued everyone. The bad-wig lady suggested ways to supplement my research income, such as providing document retrieval from the Dublin archives.

"I was thinking maybe I could offer to help people find their ancestors' homes. Do the land records go back far?"

"Ah, that they do." The lady stared at me through the red glasses on the tip of her nose. "Land records go back quite far. Start with the Tithe Applotment Books and Griffith's Valuation online. Might be able to give ya all the needed info."

I smiled, psyched to add the service to my website.

Two hours later, everyone left but Mickey. "I hope

we helped put you on the path to becoming a true genealogist."

I was inspired yet overwhelmed and a bit disheartened at how long the path was going to be.

"I'm sorry about hogging the meeting."

"Not a' tall, luv. That's what we're here for. As you can see, everyone enjoys giving advice, be it on ridding your car of pesky critters or finding ancestors. You have hundreds of years of combined experience here. Hope you'll be joining us again. And besides his cane, my cousin Nicholas left me most of his research books, if ya ever be needing to borrow one." Rather than sounding melancholy over his cousin's death, a reminiscent glint sparkled in Mickey's pale-blue eyes.

"That'd be great. He loaned me two I need to return."

"He'd be wanting ya to keep 'em."

I nodded, smiling.

I told him about my IRA visitor, but he didn't have time to help the poor guy either.

"I'd suggest he be looking in the Mullingar paper 'round the time of the bombings. Even if they occurred elsewhere, if the hideout was discovered in Killybog, it would likely have made the local paper, on microfilm at the Mullingar library. I don't recall offhand having heard about it. Yet I also don't recall whether or not I fed Stewey this morning."

A warm feeling washed over me at the thought of Mickey caring for Nicholas's rabbit, which came and went through an open window and often slept in the flower box.

"Speaking of Stewey, not sure what I'll be doing with

the wee fella once Nicholas's house sells. Can't be keeping the windows open at home with Mary being susceptible to pneumonia." He raised a curious brow.

"I'm not living in Killybog, just staying the week."

Besides, I couldn't allow the rabbit to come and go as he pleased when Mac couldn't. And how would I explain to Mac that Stewey was allowed inside when his buddy the pine marten wasn't?

The man frowned.

"I guess I could ask Declan about keeping him."

"That'd be grand."

"I wish I'd have come to these meetings sooner when Nicholas invited me."

"Ah, don't be feeling bad, luv. Nicholas joined us here today. Never missed a meeting, he didn't. And if ya ever be having a question for him, call in on him. He's right at home now, resting amongst friends he's visited for years."

Before we said our good-byes, I promised to attend future meetings. I snagged a napkin off the bar and blew my nose. Mags had ducked in back to her residence to throw in laundry, so I got a grip before she returned. I decided to take advantage of internet service while Mac was still napping.

Rachel had e-mailed, inquiring if the electricity was back on. I hadn't responded to her last half dozen e-mails. I replied that it was, but now the internet modem was acting up. True, even though it worked fine if I tossed it out the window.

The two genealogy societies cost me only sixty euros total to join. I added my member status to my website. Having a Diploma in Family History sounded impressive.

I found the ten-week class's online registration. It started in September, one night a week. Rachel had promised I'd only have to work full time during the summer until things slowed down. If I was enrolled in school, she had to let me attend. I'd tell her it was nonrefundable. Perfect.

Except that it cost a thousand euros.

I wouldn't get my final Flanagan's check for several weeks. I would need to put the class on my credit card. My chest tightened at the thought of falling back into debt. At least I'd have checks from the estate events.

As long as the actors got *hitched.*

I packed up my computer and went over to tell Mags good-bye. A sign behind the bar advertised eggs for sale. Mags raised chickens out back. I shared my chicken in the cottage story.

She laughed. "Those birds have a mind of their own, they do. Once left a bedroom window open when I ran to Tesco and returned home to find an egg in the middle of the bed."

"But no hen?"

She shook her head. "Managed to make its own way back out."

Of course it had.

"Surprised to see ya in on a weekday," she said.

"I'm staying near Killybog. Declan is a caretaker for my uncle's aunt."

"Ah, grand. Glad he found a spot. Heard he was looking at the Whelan place. Too close to the road for me. I'd be worried a car would take the corner a mite fast and end up in the living room."

The Whelan place? What was the Whelan place?

Mags added more beer to the cooler behind the bar, unaware of my wide eyes and gaping mouth.

"Would you fancy a cuppa tea?" she asked.

The Irish cure for any problem was tea. Unless I was popping a Xanax with the hot golden beverage, no way was it going to calm me down. Declan had been looking at renting a house behind my back. Or possibly *buying* a house! This was way worse than his spur-of-the-moment decision to move into the Daly house. Actually, it wasn't even spur of the moment, since he'd apparently been planning a move and had merely seized the opportunity when it arose. If I'd agreed to a larger apartment, would he still have been considering the Whelan place?

If Mags knew Declan was house hunting, had Zoe known? How about his mom? They were both at work, so I was unable to stop by their house and ask them. Besides, I couldn't put them in the middle of an awkward situation.

Yet I couldn't believe the local pub owner knew Declan was looking for a house when I hadn't!

"The couple that has been married the longest?" I posed the question to the sixty-seven attendees seated under the white pavilion tent at the clan gathering. People had mingled for a half hour, marking off the squares on their Daly bingo cards.

"Clare and Roger Daly from Wales," an older American man shouted out, once again without raising his hand.

Aldrich Whitaker Quincy Daly III.

A perfect name for the pompous ass who'd taken over the Daly clan gathering prior to, and during, the event. I'd unknowingly helped him in doing so by organizing an online forum, per his request, to get attendees psyched about the event. Big mistake. Sir Pompous helped people to connect through DNA matches and shared family trees. Everything I'd planned to do at the gathering and offer as part of my genealogy services. Only two people were unsure about their Daly connection, but not curious enough to pay my fee. So this had become more of a family reunion than a business opportunity for me.

I plastered on a smile, trying not to grit my teeth, unable to afford oral surgery. "Again, please raise your hand so everyone gets a chance to answer."

The tall, gray-haired man gave me an apologetic smile. "Sorry about that. It's just that I feel like I know everyone so well."

I wanted to call out, *Who is the most annoying know-it-all here?* But nobody would get it right. He'd already received three rounds of applause and numerous kudos for *his* assistance with the gathering. A growl vibrated at the back of my throat.

Declan flashed me an encouraging smile from the back of the tent. I held his gaze, trying to send him a psychic message. *Why didn't you tell me about the Whelan place?* He continued smiling at me, apparently not receiving my telepathic transmission. It was ridiculous that I could bring George and Fanny together. Gerry and Rachel. Mom and her half brother. George and his aunt Emily. Why couldn't I get my own relationship together?

Fanny raised her hand, and I called on her.

"I would like to announce that we've been married the shortest amount of time. We're getting married in two weeks!" She let out an excited squeal.

George gave her a kiss.

Emily smiled at the couple seated next to her. Thankfully, she didn't still seem upset that I'd allowed Liam to skulk around on her property.

The clan bingo ended. Everyone grabbed refreshments and perused the photo boards, searching for ancestors who resembled each other.

Declan strolled up looking way sexy in dark jeans, white button-down shirt, navy vest, and blue-and-gray tie. Suddenly feeling ten degrees warmer in the shaded tent, I slipped off the white sweater covering my sleeveless green sundress.

"Brilliant job." Declan brushed a kiss to my lips.

"Except no clients."

"Nobody choked on a biscuit, did they now?"

I glared at Sir Pompous. "Unfortunately not."

Declan's lips curled into an amused smile. "That arse won't be at another clan gathering. Ya did a fab job keeping your cool while keeping him in line. Your next gathering will have loads of clients."

I nodded faintly, appreciating the pep talk.

Emily joined us. "What a lovely gathering. So glad I came. And Fanny just invited me to her hen party. How exciting. I've never been to one. Been to several bridal showers, but they seem quite boring by comparison."

By comparison to *what*? I couldn't picture Emily sticking a dollar bill in a stripper's G-string. I was about to pick her brain for what a woman her age would consider exciting when she changed the topic.

"Has your visitor returned to see the house in the woods?"

Declan raised a curious brow. "Visitor?"

I filled him in on Liam. "I was going to mention it, but we barely saw each other this week."

His blue eyes sharpened. "Jaysus, Caity. What were ya thinking, going back in the woods with some bloke ya just met? Lucky thing he wasn't a crazed killer."

"I know, but my gut told me he wasn't. And the librarian and Chinese takeaway lady saw us together."

I peered over at Emily. "If he does come back, I'll ask him to leave."

I'd feel bad denying him access to his family's home, as untraditional as it was.

"Nonsense. I was quite dramatic about the whole thing. It merely took me by surprise, as did that the structure is still standing after all these years."

"It's actually in good shape." I scrolled through the pics on my phone.

Emily held up a hand. "Wait. Please go back a snap."

I went back to the previous shot of Liam in front of the abandoned hideout.

Emily's gaze narrowed on the pic. "Can you enlarge it?"

I did as she requested.

"A rather handsome bloke, isn't he now?" Declan said.

I ignored the comment, though his jealous tone was reassuring. "Does it look the same as you remember?" I asked Emily.

Her breathing quickened. "Oh my, it is in grand shape, isn't it?" She smiled faintly. "Might you e-mail me that snap?"

"Sure. That reminds me. Liam asked me to text him my pics. And since I didn't get any clients today, now I can help him find his father. Any info you have on the place would be great. I'd like to write up a homestead biography for him."

Emily placed a hand to her forehead. "I'm feeling a bit faint. I could use a spot tea and a sit in the garden."

"You go on," Declan said. "I'll fetch your tea."

"That would be lovely, dear. Milk, no sugar. I'll pay Mac a visit out back." Emily headed toward the garden.

"Not in good form, is she?" Declan said. "Quite pale. Hope she isn't ill."

I nodded. She still hadn't gained back all the weight she'd lost that spring thanks to a nasty flu.

Declan headed over to the beverage station.

Sir Pompous sidled up next to George a few feet away and gestured at a vintage photo of an older man. "You have my great-grandfather's profile." The guy rambled on, comparing George's features to his ancestor's.

George shot me a panicked look. Fanny was chatting with a group of women, unaware of his need for help. I joined him. I'd be freaking out too if I was related to that idiot. George had no interest in doing a DNA test, worried about online hackers selling his results on the black market. It had only recently become popular, or he might have done it nine years ago when he'd discovered his parents weren't his biological ones.

"Rachel is waving us over," I lied.

We made a quick getaway and joined Rachel and Gerry outside the tent, taking a break from the group. My sister wore a long red sundress with brown sandals. Her work wardrobe was becoming much more casual and colorful. Gerry had exchanged his usual bartending T-shirt and jeans for a lightweight gray sweater and black slacks. Everyone had spiffed up for the occasion except Thomas, who was working rather than attending the event. Dressed in green wellies and brown gardening trousers, he was pruning stray leaves and twigs from *Venus de Milo's* curvy topiary figure. You'd never know that sheep had trimmed off *David's* private parts months earlier.

"Now that you have business cards, I can be giving them to my mates Jimmy Reilly and Will Cavanaugh, publicans in Dublin," Gerry said. "Also have one who owns McGuire's Auto Repairs and one that runs Sweeney's Hardware in Kildare. Never know when someone might wander in one of these spots looking for a long-lost rellie by the same name."

I smiled. "Thanks."

Gerry was a keeper, though Rachel had almost screwed it up this past spring. After this weekend, they'd officially be roomies. She'd put her condo on the market and her furnishings on Craigslist. When her condo sold, she'd return to Milwaukee to close the deal and ship personal belongings. My mom was taking Rachel's move fairly well. It gave her one more reason to visit Ireland and England. Maybe when she and Dad retired, they would make the move themselves.

"I'm hiring her," George said. "Need to be tracing my ancestors back further to ensure I'm indeed not related to that buffoon."

"You did an incredible job today," Rachel said. "It sucks you didn't get any clients."

She sounded sincere rather than glad that I'd now be available to assist her full time without distractions. Surprisingly, she hadn't bombarded me with *Sunnyvale* ideas all day. Had my comment about a possible alternate ending finally dampened her optimism?

"We still made a great profit, especially with few overhead costs." I gestured to the yellow-and-blue floral-patterned linens covering the round tables Rachel had picked up for a steal when a local restaurant had closed its doors. Between that find and hitting estate sales, she'd never have to pay furniture rental fees. "Maybe this could be my niche, planning clan gatherings."

Rachel nodded faintly. "But the Daly connection to the estate probably helped attendance."

"We agreed on doing more gatherings to drum up business for me," I said firmly. "And they'd also benefit the estate."

"Besides this gathering, you haven't been really focused on your genealogy job," she said. "I know you love the research, but are you sure you want to pursue it as a career?"

Declan walked up, hearing her comment. "She built a fierce website this week and attended her first genealogy meeting."

I gave him a smile for having my back. "And I had a prospective client wanting to hire me a few days ago. Now I can help him out." I had to get more clients pronto.

"Shit." Rachel peered past me at a small van motoring up the drive, with Cousin Enid behind the wheel. Even though she wasn't furiously pedaling her usual bicycle, that foreboding music announcing the arrival of the Wicked Witch of the West played in my head.

Thomas sliced the hedge clipper blades through the air in Enid's direction. The sheep she'd let loose on the property had been responsible for *David's* private parts needing cosmetic surgery.

Enid stepped from the van. Except for no black helmet, she wore her typical riding attire—fitted tan slacks, a black blazer, and knee-high black boots.

"What are you doing here?" Rachel demanded.

Enid missed slapping a hand on her hip, throwing herself off balance. She peered at George with bloodshot eyes. "I'm here to pick up my grandmother's settee."

Her booze breath made my eyes water.

George scowled at her. "You're trolleyed."

"I certainly am not. Never been trolleyed in my life."

"Then you're ossified," Declan said. "And I'll be driving ya home."

Enid took an unsteady step toward Declan. "I'm sure you'd love to drive me home." The woman's attempt at flirting was just plain weird. Especially after a previous snide remark concerning Declan's Irish accent. "But first, my settee George promised me."

Agreeing to give her the couch had apparently been a peace offering. Was George nuts? Enid was the one who owed him an apology after she'd threatened to sue him for family heirlooms when he was lying in the hospital with pneumonia.

Enid's gray-eyed gaze narrowed on the activity in the tent. "What's going on here?"

"The Daly clan gathering," George said.

She snarled. "That's today?"

"Too bad you didn't register for it." Rachel made a shooing gesture for Enid to run along.

Sir Pompous strolled over and thrust out a hand, introducing himself. "Were you on the clan forum?"

"I'm not here for your little event." Enid abruptly squared her shoulders, once again throwing herself off balance.

"This is my cousin Enid Daly," George said.

"A Daly. Well then, you should be at the event. I'm sure Caity here can get you registered."

Enid pursed her lips. A lifetime of looking like she sucked on lemons had caused deep wrinkles around the woman's mouth. "No thank you."

"Have you taken a DNA test? If you haven't, you should." He rambled on about the DNA connections he'd made.

"Bloody hell. Leave me alone. I'm not even a Daly." Enid rocked back on her bootheels.

George grabbed hold of her arm, steadying her. "Why don't you have a seat. I'll get you some tea."

"Tea won't make me a Daly," she slurred.

Sir Pompous excused himself and escaped back to the tent.

George glared at Enid. "Must you be so rude? And was lying to the poor chap really necessary?"

Sticking up for the *poor chap* showed just how much George despised his cousin.

Enid's gaze sharpened. "I wasn't lying."

"Not a Daly?" he scoffed. "What nonsense are you trying to pull now?"

"If I say I'm not a Daly, I'm not." Her forceful tone knocked her back, her butt hitting the ground with a thud.

George and Declan helped her up.

Enid glared at me. "After you threatened to prove George was indeed a Daly by having him take a DNA test, I took the test prepared to prove he wasn't one. Only to prove *I* am not one."

Wow. Karma was a bitch. And so was Enid.

Last spring, when Mom had mentioned she and George were half siblings, Enid had made a rude remark, assuming George wasn't a Daly. She still didn't know how George and I were related.

"How did a test prove this?" George asked.

"Yes, I can't imagine George could be so lucky to not be related to you," Rachel said.

"Two Daly cousins took the same test. I'm not a match with either."

"Maybe they're the ones not Dalys," I said.

"They're from different families. When I nonchalantly questioned them on their test results, they had a DNA match with several of our, or rather, *their* second cousins. And not one person in my thirty thousand matches has the surname Daly."

This was sounding like my client Nigel's history. The thought that Enid's ancestor might turn out to be a convict shipped off to prison almost made me smile. Yet sympathy tugged at my heart. Sympathy for Enid? After eighty years, Enid discovered the name she'd identified with her entire life wasn't hers. If I learned I wasn't a Shaw, I wouldn't stop until I knew the truth. And I deserved to get at least one client out of this clan gathering.

"I can do your family research," I blurted out.

Rachel gasped in horror.

Why would I help nasty Cousin Enid?

To prove I was taking my business seriously and to not become a full-time *Sunnyvale* event planner. And because I was so desperate for money to start my business, I'd literally sell my soul to the devil himself.

I just had.

Enid raised a skeptical brow. "Why would you help me?"

"That's my job. I'm a genealogist. My hourly rate is forty euros plus expenses. Ten hours paid up front."

George nodded his approval.

Declan looked surprised. Not having the nerve to list a fee on my website, I'd offered to provide an estimate upon request.

"Around thirty-five pounds an hour," Declan said, doing the exchange rate in his head.

Not only did I not mind overcharging Enid—pain and suffering compensation—but needing to be discreet, Enid wouldn't rip me to shreds on social media if I failed. She'd merely do it in person.

I slipped a business card from my pocket.

Enid refused it. "That's outrageous. I would never pay such a fee, especially when you should be helping me for free."

"Why would I help you for free?"

"It's your fault I found out all of this nonsense in the first place."

"I'm not the one who kept a family secret from you."

"Well, I'm not paying you thirty-five pounds an hour."

I shrugged. "That's the going rate."

"And you could trust Caity to be discreet, which I should think you'd want with such a sensitive matter," George said.

"Actually, you don't know for sure it was your father and not your grandfather," I said. "This could go back generations."

Her rigid features relaxed slightly. The more removed the scandal, the better.

"Your brother Oliver should take a DNA test," George said.

Enid gasped. "Absolutely not. That is out of the question. We haven't spoken in months. I'm certainly not going to ring him and ask for his DNA."

"If you're full siblings, then you know your mother wasn't unfaithful," I said. "Actually, you don't know any ancestor was unfaithful. Maybe she wasn't married at the time."

Enid turned up her nose at such a slanderous possibility. "I'd like my settee. I have places to be."

"Why do you want the settee if you aren't a Daly?" Rachel said.

Wow, that was a low blow, even for Rachel.

"The settee!" Enid's body trembled with anger.

We all jumped.

Slag.

Even though the woman was a complete nightmare, she'd have been a dream client, paying me what I was worth.

CHAPTER ELEVEN

That night, Declan and I were sitting on the library couch next to the lit fireplace. Clichéd pep talk or I told you not to put all your eggs in one basket would have been better than the silence between us. It would also keep me from blurting out that I knew about the Whelan place. I needed to tactfully bring it up. To know if he'd wanted to leave my tiny apartment or to leave *me*.

Declan sipped whiskey from a crystal glass, studying his sketch. A couple at the gathering had contracted him to paint a family portrait, when he hadn't even been promoting his services. He'd be ready to start it when he returned to Emily's tomorrow. I snuggled into his blue wool sweater despite the fireplace heating up the room. I was brainstorming ways to obtain clients, including Liam, and was grateful for Gerry's offer to distribute my cards to his five buddies.

"An inch to the right," Rachel said, supervising Gerry's placement of Caroline and Lawrence's wedding portrait over the fireplace. "That's perfect."

Gerry nodded at Declan. "It's brilliant. Should be doing wedding portraits, ya should."

Declan glanced up from his sketch pad. "Jaysus, wouldn't want to be dealing with bridezillas demanding to look thinner, their hair longer, nose smaller. I'd go mad."

"I'll definitely have you paint my wedding portrait." Rachel blushed, avoiding Gerry's curious look.

The doorbell rang. Rachel escaped to answer it. Gerry's mesmerized gaze followed her out of the room.

Did Declan still look at me that way when I left a room?

Rachel returned to the library.

"Who was at the door?" I asked.

"Cousin Enid."

"What'd she want?"

"I didn't ask. Just shut the door in her face."

Curiosity more than common courtesy had me in the foyer opening the front door to find Enid still standing there.

She slipped a sheet of paper from a large envelope and a pen from her purse. She thrust both at me. "Here is everything you need to get started. My family tree, or at least the family tree as I *know* it. What must be my closest paternal DNA matches, seeing as they don't share matches with my maternal relatives. And my account information."

I squinted at the paper's small print. "What's this?"

"A confidentiality agreement."

I wanted to ask why the document wasn't on Edwards and Price letterhead, the solicitors' firm she'd claimed was buying the estate and handling her bogus lawsuit against George. However, I kept my yap shut, needing money and experience more than I needed to be snarky.

"I won't share your information with anyone, except Declan. He's helped me with past research. I might need his assistance."

Enid reluctantly agreed.

I wrote in his name and read the document word for word, not trusting the woman.

"If I learn you aren't discreet, I won't give you a cent."

"Speaking of which..." I gave her a knowing look.

She slipped a white envelope from her purse and handed it to me. I tore it open. She let out an offended *hrmph* as if I was rude for counting the money in front of her.

I eyed the bills. "You're a hundred short. I said thirty-five pounds an hour and ten hours paid up front. That's three hundred and fifty pounds, not two hundred and fifty."

"I can't afford thirty-five pounds an hour. Twenty-five is it. Take it or leave it."

I wanted to tell her to kiss off. But I didn't want to tell two hundred and fifty pounds to kiss off. Yet it was the principle. And if I let her walk all over me right from the get-go, I was screwed.

I held out my hand.

Enid glared at me, her lips pressed into a thin line.

I held her gray-eyed gaze and my breath.

A growl vibrated in her throat.

With a defeated grunt, she whipped open her purse and handed over five twenty-pound notes.

Wow. The first game of chicken I'd won!

I stuffed the bills into the envelope. "I'll invoice you for every twenty hours before I continue further research."

I didn't trust Enid to pay me at the end of weeks of research. I wrote on the envelope that this was the agreed-upon payment plan. She grudgingly signed it.

"What changed your mind?" I asked.

"I don't care for you. However, you are bullheaded, persistent, relentless—"

"Spunky?"

She looked unamused.

Something told me there was more to it than these favorable traits of mine.

"Besides, I already spilled the beans to you. I might as well hire you. That English chap, Nigel, sounded impressed." She turned on her heels and clomped down the steps.

A sense of pride rose inside me. Had my website testimonial really sold her on hiring me?

I returned to the library, where Gerry and Rachel were snuggling on a couch.

Rachel gestured to the envelope. "What's that?"

"Enid's family history and a cash advance."

She sprang to her feet, a wild look in her eyes. "Have you gone batshit crazy? What in the world possessed you to help that bitch?"

"Unfortunately, I don't have the luxury of discriminating against undesirable clients."

"You asked if she was serious 'bout the job," Declan said, tossing his sketchpad on the table.

Rachel glared at Declan, then over at me. "Not Enid. That woman will suck the life out of you."

"Don't worry. I'll still be able to help with *Sunnyvale* events."

"This isn't about the events. It's what she tried to do to George. Her making our lives a living hell."

Gerry placed a calming hand on Rachel's arm.

"So then it's a good thing I'm taking her money."

Our uncle walked in wearing a tan robe and slippers, having been relaxing upstairs with a book. "What's going on here?"

"Enid just hired Caity," Rachel spat.

George nodded his approval. "I'm glad that woman came to her senses."

Rachel shook her head. "Caity sure hasn't."

"Now, Rachel, business is business," he said. "I have to admit I feel a bit sorry for Enid. I know how difficult it was to learn my parents were not my biological ones, yet at least I am still a Daly."

"It's still not right." Rachel stalked out of the library.

Gerry followed, trying to cool her down.

George gave me a sympathetic smile. "I just hope you don't regret it. You know how obstinate that woman can be. But you must pursue *your* dreams, not Rachel's. The estate will be fine."

"I'll still be helping with events."

"If that's what you wish, dear." George kissed my cheek and walked out. Even though he empathized with Enid, not being related to the wretched woman had put a bounce in his step.

I plopped down on the couch next to Declan, removing Enid's paperwork from the envelope. Her family tree only went back to her great-grandparents.

My client Nigel's mom had done a DNA test attempting to confirm family lore that her grandfather had been of blue blood. Instead, she'd discovered she wasn't a hundred percent English. Nigel had hired me to learn the truth. I'd lucked out and found someone had revealed his grandpa's identity in a family tree online. He'd refused my offer to return his payment.

So I still hadn't a clue on how to conduct DNA research.

I pulled up the ancestry site and entered Enid's password, a lengthy combination of letters, numbers, and symbols. A bit paranoid about having her account hacked? My password for everything was Declan1. I was every hacker's dream. Except my bank accounts had no money to steal, and my credit limit was pathetic.

Enid's account popped up. Her profile name was Charlie.

"Charlie?" Declan said. "A bit informal for Enid."

I clicked on Ethnicity and Origins.

"Omigod," I muttered, staring at the screen.

A sly grin curled Declan's lips. "Forty-two percent Irish, is she?"

When we'd first met Enid, she'd made a nasty remark about Declan's Irish accent. What did she have against the Irish?

Except for the fact that someone in her family tree was Irish and responsible for her not being a Daly.

"The bloke might have been a blow-in from Ireland, living in England. Or had a fling while visiting here."

"He could also have been Scottish. Ireland and Scotland ethnicities are grouped together."

"It lists Leinster under Ireland, which encompasses north of Dublin down to Waterford and out to the Midlands. It doesn't break down Scotland, but that's not to say there isn't Scottish in her blood."

Enid and her maternal cousins shared mainly English ethnicity. I clicked on what Enid noted as one of her closest paternal connections, My Fair Lassie—a second-to-third cousin. "She's Irish but doesn't state her location."

"With that profile name, she's obviously a fan of musicals, Audrey Hepburn or Rex Harrison."

"Gee, that narrows it down to half the world."

Enid and Lassie shared 132 DNA matches. One of which, Rosie, was another second-to-third cousin. There were two third-to-fourth cousins, and the rest were distant. The match estimated a 63 percent chance that Lassie and Rosie were Enid's second cousins, or first cousins twice removed. I Googled a chart on plotting relationships.

"Based on this chart, Enid and these women share great-grandparents or two-time great-grandparents, depending on their generations. That's a long way back. One couple could have dozens of great-grandchildren. Maybe even a hundred, with the large families the Irish had."

None of the four closest matches had family trees linked to their profiles. Inputting Enid's tree into Ancestry.com was top priority. Even though the confidentiality agreement required the tree remain private, it would help determine her relationship with matches. Despite DNA testing, a person's tree still needed to be as complete as possible to find the connection.

My Fair Lassie had last logged in three months ago. Rosie had been two months, and the other two within the last few weeks.

"I can't wait weeks or months to hear from people. I need them to respond now. How do I write a message that they'll reply to? Should I say I'm a genealogist or just writing on Enid's behalf? They might be more responsive if they think I have a personal connection with her." I cringed at the thought. "Should I be up front that I'm researching her paternal side?"

"If the connection is further back, people mightn't care about a scandalous family secret. If it's closer, they might not respond. A bit of a touchy subject."

No matter how I worded the message, I felt bad for the people on the receiving end. Their lives were about to change, and not for the better, being related to Cousin Enid.

CHAPTER
TWELVE

The following day, Declan and I took a morning ferry from Wales to Dublin. Mac was a bit loopy from antianxiety meds, so he wouldn't wig out or puke all over Declan's car like he had his first trip abroad. *I* was going to need meds, working with Cousin Enid.

I searched online, hoping Enid's family popped up in other people's trees. Like had happened with my client Nigel. Nada. With the little info Enid had supplied, it took less than an hour to create her family tree back to her great-grandparents. Both her father, Edward Daly, and her grandfather, Albert, had been firstborns. One of them might have been conceived out of wedlock with a man other than their supposed fathers.

Unless the secret went back even further.

Enid didn't have copies of her ancestors' baptismal or marriage records so I could verify if the children were conceived after their parents' marriage. It would have been difficult to lie about a child's birthdate in a small community. I had to locate the records.

No responses from Enid's DNA matches. However, Enid had replied to my e-mail questioning her 42 percent Irish ethnicity.

I glanced over at Declan seated next to me. "According to Enid, her family's only connection to Ireland was the Daly family in Killybog. Her family lost touch with them after they moved to Ireland in the mid-eighteen hundreds. I wonder if Michael even knew his cousin, Isabella Daly, when he and my grandma went to live with her and her husband, Henry Wood, in England. And then my grandma left George in their care."

"Well, one of Enid's maternal ancestors didn't share Enid's dislike for the Irish. Would have been quite a scandal back then for an unwed woman to be pregnant, let alone with an Irish lad's baby, with all the turmoil going on."

"And even more of a scandal with such a hoity-toity family background. If her family even knew. Who's to say she was an unwed mother? Maybe this goes back even further and a woman had an affair. Enid also says her mother once mentioned an older Scottish gent visiting her mom. Enid's grandfather kicked him out of their house."

"Right, then. That might be a clue, or not."

My fried brain needed a break from the mental gymnastics, so I texted Liam that I could assist with his research in a few weeks. He responded with a slew of celebratory emojis. I slipped my credit card from my wallet and filled Declan in on the ten-week class Mickey had mentioned.

"I'm going to register right now." Rather than anxiety over going in debt, my stomach fluttered with anticipation at taking a step forward in my career.

Declan smiled. "That's grand."

After signing up for the class, I went in search of caffeine. I passed by a gift shop displaying *Sunnyvale* T-shirts, mugs, shopping bags, and trinkets.

My body tensed. Even hundreds of miles at sea, there was no escaping the hype.

A ding signaled a text. Rachel.

Talk about freaky timing.

My sister apologized for not having been up this morning to say good-bye. Although she didn't approve of Enid as a client, she wanted me to suck every dime I could out of the wretched woman. She also wondered what I thought about a clan gathering with Caroline and Lawrence. That I could trace their ancestry so people with the same surnames could hire me to verify if they were related.

At least this idea was related to my genealogy research. Rachel's idea of a compromise? I had to admit, it was one of her better ones.

❦ ❦

Declan parked down the street from Coffey's pub. I hooked Mac's collar to his leash while Declan grabbed my suitcase from the trunk. An icky feeling tossed my tummy at the thought of Declan leaving and me being alone in my apartment. Of his plans to rent the Whelan house without telling me. At the thought of Grandma being separated from Michael due to his early death. And Enid's pregnant ancestor not being with the father of her child...

Mac whimpered, yanking on his leash, attempting to head back toward the car.

With my fall classes and lectures, I wasn't going to be able to stay at Emily's often. And Declan would be traveling in another week. I needed to be at the house when he was there so we could continue smoothing things over. That weekend had gone well. I wanted to maintain the momentum.

"We're going with you to Emily's," I blurted out, coming to an abrupt halt.

Declan smiled, a curious glint in his blue eyes.

"Why don't you take Mac for a walk while I pack?"

He gave me a kiss, then he and Mac strolled off down the sidewalk.

Should I pack my large suitcase, a carry-on, or both? I wasn't sure, but at least I was headed in the right direction. Even if it was to the Daly home, it was with Declan. Thankfully, he'd chosen Emily's over Whelan's. Being near Grandma's home was inspiring and comforting. If any place could help me make things right, it was there.

❧ ☙

When we neared Emily's, Declan slowed down for a woman in a yellow rain slicker running down the road, flapping her arms, attempting to chase a hen back to a fenced-in flock.

Mac peered over my shoulder from the backseat, growling at the chicken scurrying down the road.

Declan laughed. "Ah, the visitor from your granny's house, no doubt."

"Must not have stopped by today, or it would still be in the cottage squawking to get out. Good to know where it lives."

We arrived at Emily's to find a small white car blocking part of the drive's entrance.

"Arse," Declan muttered. He unlocked the gate and maneuvered our vehicle around the car, just missing it.

We headed up the drive toward a man snooping around the side of the house.

I rolled my eyes. "That's Mattie. The Tidy Town man. He must have scaled the gate to check our progress and reprimand me for slacking off on rubbish duty."

"Jaysus. I was only home a day between work and England. What a bloody pain."

The nosey man greeted us with a grim look. No friendly hello or apology for blocking the drive and trespassing.

"Someone dug up my bushes, nicked my hanging baskets of petunias and pansies."

Declan gestured to the dead bushes and overgrown weeds and grass. "It wasn't us."

"They nicked mine because they're too cheap and lazy to buy their own. Knew I'd replace 'em."

They'd likely swiped them to keep him busy worrying about his own landscaping and his nose out of everybody else's.

"I'll get started on the yard work straight away," Declan said.

"Much appreciated. And I'd appreciate any info you might hear on the thief who nicked mine. Don't be forgetting about rubbish collection. Your road is looking a bit sketchy." He marched down the drive in hot pursuit of the flower thieves.

"He'll undoubtedly be cruising by tonight to confirm we're doing our part," I said. "Next to the Tidy Town distinction on village signs, they should include a memorial to the residents picked off while risking their lives for the sake of the cause."

Smiling, Declan slipped an arm around my shoulders. I relaxed against him. "Sunny and seventy, perfect weather for planting." He eyed the front of the house. "What color shrubs would ya fancy?"

"How about pink, purple, and cream-colored pom-pom bushes like at George's estate?"

"Grand. Should I also be getting some tall shrubs and try my hand at topiary? Sculpt a few dogs or nude statues?"

"Thomas would be proud." I gave him a kiss. "Oh, and pick up a welcome mat. People need to be wiping off their feet before going inside. I'm tired of sweeping up mud."

"Sure ya want people to be calling in? You might never get Enid's research done."

"Oh, I'll get it done."

"What color for the gate?"

"Green. I've always dreamed of having a green fence. And can you also pick up some chicken treats?"

"Chicken-flavored dog treats?"

"No, like treats for chickens. I'm guessing there's such a thing."

Wearing a curious smile, Declan slid into the car and drove off. A serene feeling washed over me.

We were already more in sync.

With an overwhelming sense of optimism, I went inside to work on Enid's research. A few hours later, I'd located her parents', grandparents', and great-grandparents' marriage records. They'd all been married in the same church as Michael and Grandma, near George's. Enid's dad and granddad were firstborns, ten to eighteen months after their parents' weddings. Could they have fabricated a document? What if they'd gone away to have the child, then lied about the birthdate?

If the infidelity had occurred further back than Enid's grandpa, and during the marriage, that would make things much more difficult. Enid's great-grandparents' marriage record provided the couples' fathers' names. With the help of the census, I could go back another generation if needed. My Fair Lassie and Rosie might be connected through two-time great-grandparents. I needed to review one of their family trees.

I e-mailed Enid, asking if she knew the relationship of the witnesses and sponsors in the marriage and baptismal records. No clue if that info would be helpful, but I was in a holding pattern until Enid's DNA matches responded. And it would prove that I was earning my fee.

Needing a quick break to rest my eyes from the computer, I plopped down onto the couch with Emily's old photo album. How sad that the vintage family photos were left here to grow moldy in the damp house.

At least she hadn't sold them to an antique store or tossed them away.

I paged through the black-and-white pics, hoping my Coffey home had photobombed a shot. In one photo, two young couples in front of Emily's house were dressed in fancier clothes than Grandma and her sister in my photo. Wondering if the women had described their outfits like Grandma had, I looked at the back. It was dated 1909 with the names *Polly*, *Nellie*, *Richard S.*, and *John D.* No clothing description. I set the album on the table and went back to work.

Needing to become a DNA expert, I did some research. I discovered a website that allowed all three major DNA companies' tests to be downloaded to that one site. Bonus. A good chance I might find a closer relative who'd taken a test from one of the other companies.

I was downloading Enid's DNA to the site when a car door slammed. Mac hopped off the couch and ran to the window. I peeked outside to see Declan heading toward the backyard with several bags, his car packed with colorful shrubs.

Enid's DNA file finished downloading. The results would be available in a few days.

What a waiting game!

A loud pounding came from the backyard.

Curious, Mac and I joined Declan where he was hanging a tiny purple door on a nail at the bottom of a massive oak tree. A sign on the door read, *Sshh. Fairies sleeping.*

"The door opens, but I don't want to be waking 'em if the pounding hasn't already." Declan smiled.

Mac sniffed a whimsical metal teapot painted in vivid pinks, blues, and purples decorated with ladybugs and flowers. Green signs on a straw-size post pointed the way to the Magic Wishing Pond, Fairy Passage, and Unicorn Stables. A small purple fairy stood in a yellow teacup, her elbows resting on the cup's rim.

A lump of emotion lodged in my throat. Was the fairy garden Declan's way of asking me to stay at Emily's without *asking* me?

"Thought you might like the whole tea theme." Declan handed me a tiny glass corked jar containing pink sparkly glitter. "Fairy dust to sprinkle over the garden. Supposedly pink dust helps hide fairies so they can go about their work during the day without being bothered. Thought out back would be a quiet spot to make your wishes come true."

"I...love them." A tear trailed down my cheek.

Declan wrapped me in his arms. "What's wrong?"

I cried against his shoulder, drooling on his white T-shirt. "Are...we..." I choked back a sob. "...okay?"

Declan kissed the side of my face, brushing a gentle hand over my hair. "I hope we are. I love you. I'm glad ya decided to move in here."

Move in here?

I drew back slightly and peered into Declan's dreamy blue eyes through a glassy haze. I wasn't going to ruin the moment by telling him I couldn't move in here with everything I had coming up this fall in Dublin. And I wasn't quite ready to admit I was accepting the fact that he was staying at the Daly house. Even though he hadn't confided in me about the Whelan place, I was glad he'd chosen Emily's instead.

I smiled. "I love you too."

He pulled me snugly against him and kissed me despite my blubbering. I wrapped my arms around his neck and ran my fingers through his hair, inhaling his rain-scented shampoo. I was ready to tear off his clothes right in front of Mac and the fairies when the sound of a throat clearing startled me. I wanted to douse us in pink pixie dust, making us invisible.

We reluctantly loosened our embrace.

Zoe stood there in jeans and a pink top. Her eyes widened at my pathetic appearance. "Bloody hell. Are you all right?"

I wiped the tears from my cheeks. "Just having a moment."

"Sorry my timing is shite. Was just stopping to say hi. I'll call in later."

I shook my head, even though I wanted to be alone with Declan. "Like my new fairy garden?"

"Ahh, lovely, isn't it? Our auntie Maeve had a fairy garden. She used to serve us tea in it when we were little. Of course, Declan refused to wear a fairy costume."

"Just because it was blue didn't make it manly. The only thing manly 'bout the garden was the wee stone pub with a side tower looking like a pint of Guinness. And a small troll statue flashing his bum, holding a sign, *Kiss the Blarney Stone*."

"Declan would pretend his tea was whiskey and he was knocking back pints at the pub. Our auntie didn't mind."

"Seeing as she had whiskey in her teacup."

We all laughed. Zoe's stories always gave fun insight into Declan's past and made me feel like I'd known them both longer than just months.

"A fairy garden down in Offaly holds the world record for the largest fairy gathering," Zoe said. "It's a fundraising event. Everyone dresses up, even the pets. It's quite mad but great craic. And brilliant for business." Zoe shared pics of Quigley modeling a colorful knitted fairy-winged cap. The cat looked like he could use some pink fairy dust to disappear.

Poor Quigley.

"Fancy a cuppa tea out here?" Zoe asked. "If Declan is more secure with his manliness, he can drink tea instead of whiskey."

He certainly didn't need to prove his manliness to me. I went warm all over recalling all the times Declan had proved just how manly he was. If I lost him, I feared I'd be back to eating containers of frosting and not showering for weeks.

"You two can be having tea while I unload the car." Declan headed out the fence's gate toward the front of the house.

I peered over at Zoe. "Did last night's date go better?"

She glanced down at her white flip-flops. "Not really."

"What do you mean, not really?"

She shrugged. "Nothing much to talk about." Her pink cheeks turned a crimson color.

My gaze narrowed. "Spill. What happened?"

She fidgeted with her blond ponytail.

"I can't believe you aren't going to tell me."

My hurt tone sent her on a guilt trip, and she reluctantly slid her gaze to mine. "Fine. The date sucked as usual, so I stopped at Carter's for a pint and watched the lads play darts. Sat and talked with Carrig for a bit. Got ossified and was going to walk home, but he offered me a lift. He drove me home, we had sex in his lorry, and I went to bed. I should probably be getting home." She took a step toward the gate, and I grasped hold of her arm.

"Carrig? Who's Carrig?"

Zoe bit down on her lower lip, stifling an embarrassed grin.

I gasped, sucking in so much air I nearly choked. "Carrig the sheepherder?"

She nodded.

When Declan was ten, he'd painted a Monet landscape on their neighbor Carrig's favorite sheep. So this past Christmas, when someone had dyed his sheep's wool red and green, he'd suspected Declan. My first encounter with Carrig had been when I was standing on the road baaing, trying to lead his escaped sheep back into the field. He'd thought I was a crazy Yank.

Zoe glanced over her shoulder. "Declan finds out, he'll go mad. He hates the wanker. So do I." Her tone was far from convincing. "He was a great listener but just a one-night stand. Nothing more." Her cheeks were now flaming red.

"The sex was awesome, wasn't it?"

"Of course not." Her breathing quickened. "Besides, nothing could ever come of it. I won't be living on a sheep farm next to my parents."

I didn't mention the fact that she currently lived *with* her parents.

"Promise you won't tell Declan, or anyone."

I nodded, still dumbfounded. "But what if Carrig can't keep a secret?"

"Keep what a secret?" Declan asked, carrying a potted plant into the backyard.

Panic seized Zoe's face, and her eyes darted around as she scrambled for a response.

"That he found out who dyed his sheep," I said.

"As if anyone cares who dyed the arse's sheep."

Zoe shrugged. "Was just a rumor that it was a friend of his, but he isn't telling who. I must crack on. Lots to do." Zoe flew from the backyard.

Even if she hadn't sworn me to secrecy, I wouldn't have told Declan. If he found out Carrig had shagged his sister in their parents' driveway, who knew what he'd be painting on the man's sheep. I didn't want to be responsible for sheep trotting around displaying obscene remarks on their wool coats.

❧ ☙

Next time I caught someone tossing rubbish out their car window, I was taking down the license plate number and calling the garda. I regretted volunteering to do garbage patrol so Declan could paint the gate. I'd rather be high on paint fumes than inhaling the stench of last week's deli specials from Tesco and half-eaten takeaway. My top lip curled back while I dropped a discarded pizza box in the large black garbage bag. Thankfully, I'd worn Declan's gardening gloves.

Emily's driveway was just around the bend when a mangy looking fox bolted out of the ditch, startling me. He snarled, revealing his sharp teeth, his beady eyes glued to my bag. Like Aunt Dottie when she was on one of her fad diets and I walked in with a Big Mac and fries. He probably smelled the rotting food. I held my breath. The fox took a step toward me, snarling, his teeth appearing bigger. I whipped the bag across the road and into the ditch. The fox flew over and attacked it, spoiled food flying everywhere. Two hours of garbage pickup shot to hell.

Better the garbage than me.

I raced around the corner and past Declan painting the gate. Rather than stopping to explain, I kept running up the drive, yelling over my shoulder, "Fox!" I left Declan in my dust. I blew past the pink-and-purple pom-pom bushes planted in the front and around through the back gate. I dropped down onto the wooden chair in my fairy garden, trying to catch my breath.

Declan appeared. "Jaysus, what happened? Where's the rubbish bag?"

"From here to Killybog by now." I gave him an abbreviated version of my encounter with the fox.

"Never seen ya run like that before. Was gonna holler 'Run, Forrest, run,' but thought you mightn't find it funny. I'll go down in a bit and clean up the rubbish."

"No, let Militant Mattie lose a limb over it. Besides, we've almost whipped this house into Tidy Town material in a matter of a day." I eyed the flat with leftover flowers Declan hadn't needed for the end of the drive. "Could I plant those at my grandma's? It doesn't seem right that the Daly house should make my Coffey home look even shabbier."

"That's grand. I'm going to finish the gate."

I grabbed a spade and grass clippers from the shed and the small package of chicken treats Declan had picked up. My top lip curled back at the disgusting dried larvae in the clear package that read *Mealworms*. I headed down the drive with the flowers. I peeked inside the cottage's window. No chicken. Crap. I was psyched to try my plan even though the thought of touching the treats made me gag.

After clipping the tall grass and weeds along the front of the stone cottage, I planted the flowers on each side of the weathered wooden door. Once Declan got caught up with Emily's place, I'd see if he could fix the hinges so the door would hang properly. If there was green paint left from the gate, I'd spruce up the door.

I went up to Emily's and exchanged my jeans for flannel jammie bottoms. Sipping a cup of tea, I sat at the desk, smiling down at the Coffey cottage's brightly colored flowers for several minutes before checking e-mail.

Enid had responded that she hadn't a clue who the sponsors and witnesses were for the baptismal and marriage records. It was hard to get upset over her lack of family knowledge when mine had been even worse. At least she replied quickly. Even if her responses were useless, I knew it right away.

Dusk settling in, Declan came inside and went to close the windows and drapes.

"Don't. I'll lose internet service. The modem is on the ground."

He glanced out the window. "Right, then. Need to be looking into broadband."

"Do you think Emily will pay for it?"

"If she won't, I will. This is mad. Will be costing loads more to keep replacing modems banjaxed by critters and rain." He went over and resumed working on my favorite painting—a woman seated at a desk writing a letter in a sun-filled room.

An e-mail from Fanny popped into my inbox, with a photoshopped picture of her and Caroline in blue-and-white-gingham aprons on the front of a scone's package. Fanny looked a half foot taller and thirty years younger. The woman's baked goods had received rave reviews from attendees at Caroline's fundraiser. Fanny planned to sell her scones mix at the *Sunnyvale* events.

Fanny was turning out to be quite the entrepreneur.

Remembering the hen party, I shot a message off to Mom, curious about the plans. Had I not heard from her because she didn't have any ideas or she didn't wish to share them? I suggested the CSI event Seamus had mentioned and T-shirts that read *CSI Dalwick*.

I checked on Ancestry.com to find one of Enid's third-to-fourth cousin matches had responded to my message. My heart raced. However, the woman didn't have a family tree or knew her relationship to Enid. I dropped back against the couch in frustration. Then recalling she was also a match to My Fair Lassie and Rosie, I asked if she knew them.

Within minutes she responded that she had Lassie's e-mail and would contact her about my message.

Yay! One step closer.

However, patience was a virtue I did not possess.

CHAPTER THIRTEEN

The next morning Declan made another garden-center run to pick up pots, flowers, and hanging plants for the sides of Emily's front door. We decided to stick with the purple, pink, and cream flowers for Emily's house and red and yellow ones for Grandma's. The perky colors reminded me of Grandma's sunny-yellow kitchen from when I was little. Making home improvements was fun when you weren't spending your own money. However, Declan's fairy garden had been a gift I could take with me wherever we went.

My stomach tightened at the thought of telling Declan I wasn't moving into Emily's. Yet he was the one who'd insisted I dedicate more time to my genealogy business. Between classes, lectures, genealogical society meetings, I had to be in Dublin. Splitting my time between here and my apartment should make him happy. Right?

Sitting in the garden drinking tea, wearing Declan's blue wool sweater, I texted Zoe.

You doing okay about Carrig?

After a few minutes, she responded. *No worries. I'm grand.*

You slept with him again, didn't you?

Radio silence. Omigod. Never in my wildest dreams would I have imagined Zoe with Carrig. What if it ended up being more than great sex?

I refreshed the inbox for Enid's Ancestry account every five minutes. Not nearly as anxious as I was, Mac snoozed on the ground next to me. In the distance a tractor hummed, cows mooed, and sheep baaed. I relaxed back in the chair, admiring my fairies...

Mac's eyes shot open. His ears perked up. His gaze darted to a brown furry snout and two beady eyes peeking under a wooden fence post. The pine marten. Mac raced over as the weasel slipped under the fence and into the yard. Mac let out a bark. Like a starting gun at a racetrack, they were off, running laps around the yard. I sprang to my feet and snatched the fairy teacup, metal teapot, and sign off the ground and set them on the table.

"Stop it right now!" I clapped my hands.

The weasel used the table as a launchpad to a low-lying tree branch, sending my teacup flying. The cup landed, and the fairy's head rolled across the ground. Omigod! I flew over to the decapitated fairy. The critter raced along a branch and hopped onto the fence. It scampered along the top until it reached the corner, then leapt off into the field. Mac barked, jumping against the fence.

"Mac, stop it!"

He kept barking.

I held the teacup fairy in one hand, her head in the other. "Look what you did to Mommy's fairy!"

Mac's puppy eyes pleaded with me to let him out to play with his new buddy. If I wasn't so ticked off, I'd feel bad that I was unable to explain why he couldn't be friends with the weasel. It reminded me of Mom not allowing me to play with Brittney Byers because she'd had cable and her parents were never home. Taking a calming breath, I counted to ten like Rachel always did when she was upset.

I went inside and glued on the fairy's head. I took it back out and peered around the yard for a safe spot. Unable to find one, I set it on the table for the time being.

Mac paced in front of the fence, whimpering.

A twitching pink nose and whiskers slipped under the same post the pine marten had jumped from.

Mac's gaze narrowed on it.

Two beady red eyes appeared.

Stewey?

The rabbit stared at us, nose twitching.

I walked over for a better look. The frightened rabbit attempted to flee, getting stuck. Stewey's back was wedged tightly between the fence and the ground. I grabbed the garden spade from the table and started digging around the panicked rabbit. Mac joined me, digging up the other side. If Stewey didn't stop struggling to free himself, he was going to get hurt. Heart racing, I dug faster. Finally having enough wiggle room, the rabbit escaped. Mac and I peered under the fence, panting.

No Stewey.

Mickey had apparently taken my offer to *ask* Declan about adopting Stewey as a green light to drop off the rabbit. What was I going to do? If I kept the windows open wide enough for the plump rabbit to enter, I'd have every pine marten in a fifty-mile radius in the house. And leaving food in the backyard might attract that mangy fox.

What if Stewey was too traumatized to return?

I went inside to the nearly empty fridge. Lunch meat, a few red grapes, and a half-eaten sub sandwich. My diet wasn't healthy enough for a rabbit. I put the sub's lettuce, tomatoes, and cucumbers on a napkin. I went out and slipped the food under the fence, hoping Stewey found it before the other animals did.

Mac sniffed under the fence while I sat and gulped down my tea. I propped my computer on my lap and refreshed the messages to find My Fair Lassie had responded. She was managing the DNA account for her mother, who'd died last year. She didn't have a family tree. However, her mother had left boxes of family info. I was welcome to visit her up in Donegal.

Maybe the boxes contained family letters like Grandma and her sister had written back and forth between the US and Ireland. But unlike Grandma's, they'd include last names and addresses. Aunt Teri—the hoarder—had kept the letters and Grandma's naturalization papers.

I shot the woman an e-mail, asking if today would work for a visit. If she was allergic to dogs. I couldn't leave Mac unsupervised at Emily's for an entire day. I asked her name so I wouldn't have to keep calling her Lassie and her phone number for when I got lost. That was a given. Declan's GPS was broken. He had an internal GPS radar and didn't need one. Donegal was located in northwest Ireland. Could I make the drive in a day? Could I drive it at all? I'd just driven for the first time since my England meltdown. During the few kilometers to the library, I'd scratched up the passenger door. Suddenly I was brave enough to navigate the roads halfway across Ireland?

I called Declan and excitedly relayed the woman's message. He estimated the drive to Donegal was three hours one way. He insisted on taking me. I felt bad since he was busy painting and landscaping. At least he'd made enough of a dent to keep Mattie off our backs for a while. And the man should be impressed that we were also sprucing up my Coffey home, since it was closer to the road and more visible.

I e-mailed Enid and told her of our trek to Donegal, psyched about the possible clues in this woman's boxes of family history. I pointed out my ability to get a speedy response when Lassie hadn't checked her account in three months. Besides building up Enid's confidence in me, I needed to build up my self-confidence.

Squawking carried through the quiet morning.

My visitor had returned.

I sprang from my chair and told Mac to behave while I was gone. I shut the gate to the backyard and went inside to grab the disgusting chicken treats.

When I arrived at Grandma's, I poked my head through the window. The hen stood perched on the brick in front of the door. I opened the bag of dried larvae, and my top lip curled back. I should have grabbed the gardening gloves. Cringing, I gazed up at the lovely blue sky, plucking a worm from the bag. I tossed it onto the dirt floor between me and the bird. It waddled over and gobbled up the treat. I gagged. The chicken looked up at me. I tossed another one onto the ground in front of the window. It inhaled the worm and stared expectantly at me. Taking an encouraging breath, I snatched another treat from the bag and placed it on the window frame. The chicken's clawed foot scratched the ground.

"If you want this treat, you need to hop up and get it. I am not touching another one of these wretched things until you do." I patted the windowsill. "Come on. You can do it. Don't chicken out."

It squawked at my play on words.

I gave the windowsill another pat and the chicken an encouraging pep talk. Mac was going to feel pretty silly if a chicken could be trained but he couldn't.

It waddled back over and perched on the brick.

"You were so close. You took two steps forward, then one step back. You can do it."

I told the chicken Rachel's inspirational story about the guest speaker who'd climbed Mount Everest. How the journey to the summit was a series of hikes up and down the mountain so your body slowly became acclimated with the lower oxygen levels toward the top. The point was that a setback wasn't a failure and it was often necessary to move forward. Like my genealogy research.

"So don't give up just because you took a step backward."

The bird's squawking grew louder, bored with Chicken Training 101.

"Fine. I'm going to be leaving for the day. If you return, you are on your own. That's why you need to learn to be self-sufficient, independent."

I opened the door. Rather than waddling off toward the gate, it flew off the ground, catching my leg with a claw, its beak going for the treats.

"Ouch. Stop that." I placed a hand against my outer thigh, hoping it wasn't bleeding. "Why couldn't you have flown like that out the window?"

It flew up again. I thrust out a hand, running toward the open gate. The chicken raced after me. I tossed a treat onto the side of the road. The bird ran out. I slammed the gate shut.

"No more treats!" I yelled as it waddled down the road.

That was it. I was done having my dog and a rogue chicken doing as they pleased. I'd have plenty of time to read that dog training book on the ride to Donegal.

I need some semblance of control here.

Lassie, aka Tara, confirmed today was good for a visit. I packed a bag with Mac's water bowl, treats, food, toys, long leash—should he need to be tied up outside—and pink sweater in case it got cool. It was like packing a baby's diaper bag, except Mac likely required more stuff.

Mac and I sat on the front stoop ready to go when Declan returned. We quickly unloaded hanging plants, ceramic pots, and flats of colorful flowers from the car. Within five minutes we were on the road to Donegal.

Within five *miles* I'd crawled into the backseat because Mac insisted on being Declan's wingman. He wouldn't sit still and kept pressing a paw into my chicken injury. I'd put antibiotic ointment and a Band-Aid on the scratch. Hopefully, it didn't become infected. I didn't care to explain that one to a doctor, and my travel insurance was pathetic. I needed to research insurance.

Mac on my lap also made it impossible for me to read the dog training book.

Most of the drive to Donegal was on wide roads with traffic zipping along. After studying Enid's family tree, I read several chapters of my book. According to the dog trainer, I had to stop expressing negative commands like *don't do that*, *no*, and *shut up*. The only thing I'd done right was stashing away all of Emily's valuables so Mac couldn't destroy them. Dog training would begin with feeding time tomorrow.

Nearing our destination, we turned down a one-lane road with houses on one side, the Atlantic on the other. I hung out the back window, snapping pics of the spectacular views of the bay opening into the ocean Grandma had sailed across to America.

Three bars popped up on my phone, so I checked e-mail to find ones from Enid and Rachel. Besides no kudos on my super sleuthing skills, Enid refused to pay my mileage to Donegal. She offered me ten pounds for petrol. As if I were a high school kid on an allowance. That wasn't how expenses worked. I'd hold Tara's info hostage until Enid paid me. Rachel's message confirmed that the local theater's actors were on board to reenact Caroline and Lawrence's wedding. She'd hold off buying guest favors until closer to the events.

Until the episode at the estate aired, confirming they were indeed married? I didn't even want to imagine the disappointment for Rachel, George...everyone, if they didn't get hitched.

Tara's two-story stone home was painted a light gray, on a hill overlooking the Atlantic. I stepped from the car expecting a strong ocean breeze to whip my hair against my face, but it was a calm day. A dog barked behind a wire fenced-in area on the side of the house. Mac went running over to say howdy.

Tara came out and greeted us. In her mid-forties, she had short blond hair and was dressed in teal yoga pants, a white sweatshirt, and tennies.

"Would it be okay if Mac played with your dog?"

She smiled. "That's grand. They're already fast friends." She opened the gate, and Mac ran inside the yard. The dogs sniffed each other, then raced off.

Tara led us through the house, decorated in Zen gray and blue tones. *Sunnyvale* was blaring on the living room TV.

My back muscles tightened.

She clicked the remote, and the characters disappeared.

My shoulders slowly relaxed.

The place was tidy except for the conservatory overlooking the ocean. Stacks of old scrapbooks with fraying pages sat on a white table. Six boxes contained loose newspaper clippings—news articles, wedding, birth and death announcements—postcards from Ireland attractions over the years, vintage photos...

My heart raced.

It would take forever to sift through it all.

"My granny used to make my mum and her siblings sit at the kitchen table each weekend and cut out news clippings about family and friends to paste in scrapbooks. My mum carried on the tradition for several years after she was married, but as you can see, not everything made it into books." Tara gazed longingly at the materials documenting her family history. "Unfortunately, none of us kids had an interest in sorting through everything until a few years ago when my mum's health and mind were failing." Her blue eyes watered.

I placed a hand on Tara's arm, consoling her with the story of how I hadn't even known Grandma was from Ireland until less than a year ago. Thankfully, I still had Mom to ask questions. Her limited knowledge had helped me trace our Coffeys. What else should I be asking Mom? My chest tightened at the thought of one day no longer being able to pick up the phone and ask her questions. I needed to make her a list of questions!

"I'll put the kettle on if you'd like to start scanning or taking snaps."

Scanning? Snaps?

She obviously noticed my deer-in-the-headlights look. "Sorry. Don't want the stuff to be leaving the house. If anything happened to it, I'd never forgive myself."

She walked out, and my gaze darted to Declan. "It'll take us weeks and way more phone memory to scan all of this." However, no way was I allowing Enid to rip on me or, even worse, not pay me if I didn't find her answers. The wretched woman would probably want to split the cost of research with Tara, since I was tracing her family tree in the process.

Declan gave me an encouraging smile. "Can get a B and B if she's okay with us returning tomorrow."

"Will they accept Mac?"

"I'm sure one will."

"And I'm sure Enid will refuse to pay for it."

"Screw Enid. She'll pay if she wants the information."

This research better not end up *costing* me money.

When Tara returned with tea and biscuits, I was looking at a black-and-white photo from a box—a mother and two young barefooted kids outside a thatched-roof cottage.

"Where was this taken?" I handed her the photo.

"My granny's house when she was young. Feel awful I don't know my great-granny's first name. Her married name was Byrne. In the 1911 census, there were nearly four thousand Byrnes in County Wicklow."

"I had a granny Byrne," Declan said. "There's loads of 'em."

"My grandpa William wasn't born until 1912. He must have married my granny before 1935, because my mum and her twin sister, Grainne, were born in 1936."

"Granya." I repeated the name phonetically. "That's pretty."

Tara continued staring at the pic.

"Don't be so hard on yourself for not knowing your great-grandma's name. You will." I gave her a reassuring smile. "I don't have any pics of my great-grandma and only one of my grandma in Ireland, with her sister. I've made copies in case anything happens to the original. I'd be devastated."

Tara smiled, placing the photo on the table. "Sorry again for not having a family tree. About six months ago,

I had contact with a third-cousin DNA match in the US. She sent me her tree, which is private on Ancestry.com. It had over five thousand names, but I couldn't find my family members. It was overwhelming. I'm unable to locate her message with the tree's link, but here's her e-mail address." She handed me a slip of paper. "Her Ancestry profile is Rosie."

Rosie was Enid's closest DNA connection. She hadn't responded to my message on Ancestry.com. Maybe she'd respond more quickly to an e-mail.

Tara sat at the table, cradling a china teacup in her hands. "So where do we start?"

"How about I show you Enid's tree and see if any names jump out at you?" I connected my laptop to Tara's Wi-Fi.

After studying the tree, she said none of the names sounded familiar.

"Why don't you tell me what family history you know? Are you okay if I record this?"

"Brilliant idea. I'll do the same." She slipped a phone from her sweatshirt pocket.

I recorded what little Tara knew about her Byrne family history, including dates, names, and tidbits, like her grandpa had been a miner. She didn't know many family facts, but she'd remembered many of her grandma's stories about growing up in Wicklow. Like her grandma walking to school with hot baked potatoes in her coat pockets, the hand warmers also serving as her lunch. Not only were the stories interesting, but they might hold clues we weren't aware of at the moment. I became so enthralled in her storytelling, I lost track of time.

"We should start scanning," Declan said.

I glanced at the clock on the wall. We'd been there two hours. "We're thinking we'll get a B and B tonight and come back tomorrow to do more scanning if that's okay."

Tara eyed the boxes, biting down on her lower lip. "You know what—take all this with you. You seem to respect the importance of family history. I trust ya to take good care of it. You're much more likely to piece it together than I am. Two weeks be long enough, would it?"

I smiled. "That'd be wonderful. And I promise to guard it with my life." Mac wouldn't be allowed in the peach room unsupervised for two weeks.

My phone dinged the arrival of an e-mail. Enid.

Tara went to check on the dogs while I read the message. After giving it more thought, Enid decided that Mary Daly, sponsor for Enid's dad's baptism, might have been *Polly* Daly, her grandpa's sister. She'd only known her great-aunt by her nickname. Polly was a nickname for Mary?

Polly...

"Omigod," I muttered.

"What's wrong?" Declan asked.

"Nothing. This might be good." I relayed Enid's e-mail. "Emily's album has a photo with women named Polly and Nellie—possibly a nickname for Eleanora, Enid's grandma? I need to e-mail Enid the photo and confirm the women's identities. If Nellie was Enid's grandma, what had she been doing at the Daly Estate when her English family supposedly had no contact with their rellies in Ireland?"

Declan nodded. "So the liaison with an Irish bloke may have happened in Ireland, not England."

"I don't remember the names of the two guys in the pic. One of them might have been Enid's mysterious biological grandfather. But I can't jump to conclusions until she confirms the woman was indeed her grandma."

I couldn't wait to take another look at Emily's photo.

The drive back to Emily's seemed to take forever. Not only because I was anxious to see the photo, but I was squished in the backseat between stacks of scrapbooks and boxes. Of course, now that Mac wasn't allowed to sit in back with the fragile materials, he sat in front whimpering that he no longer wanted to play wingman. Finishing that dog training book was a top priority. Yet if we both became overwhelmed with how much Mac had to learn, we might give up. One step at a time.

We arrived at home just after nine. I raced into the house, deactivated the alarm, and zipped into the peach room. I removed the pic from the photo album and read the back. *Polly, Nellie, James D.*, and *Richard S.* Emily could likely confirm that the D. was for Daly. Who was Richard S.? The photo was dated 1909. One year before Enid's father was born.

My heart raced.

Nellie had to be Enid's grandma.

I snapped a shot and sent the photo off to Enid, asking her to identify the women and if the guys' names were familiar. I also sent it to Emily, hoping she'd confirm James D. was her brother. Nicholas Turney had mentioned a James Daly when assisting me with my research at Christmastime. Fingers crossed Emily would know Richard S.'s identity. Since she'd left family photo albums in a musty house, she wouldn't mind me snooping through them. Right?

I scanned the rest of the album and two others, finding three more pics of James D., but none of Richard S. Desperate to learn their last names, I pulled up Ireland's 1911 census on my laptop. I found several James Dalys. None lived in Killybog. Unable to search a surname with merely an initial, I searched all Richards in Westmeath. There were 336 of them, but only a handful with the last name starting with S. Yet Killybog was near the County Meath and Cavan borders. He could have been from either of those counties, or visiting from another country, like Scotland! Again, before I wasted hours investigating, I needed Enid to confirm that was indeed her grandma in the photo.

If Byrne hadn't been such a common name, I'd merely trace Tara's family back. Hoping maybe she'd missed a tree online, I searched but came up empty. I shot an e-mail off to Rosie—with over five thousand names in her tree—hoping that she'd forward it within the next day and a name would jump out at me.

Declan had unloaded the car. We stared at the overwhelming amount of information sitting on the table.

"Would be easiest to start with what's already organized in the scrapbooks," I said. "Maybe we'll luck out and not have to delve into the chaotic boxes."

He nodded, grabbing a scrapbook.

"It's going to take us a hundred hours to sift through all of this. Enid's never going to pay that, especially if I come up empty. A good thing I'm billing her every twenty hours. My website needs to state that I'll be paid in full for my research time regardless of what info is found. Maybe I can add a button to accept the terms and conditions."

At 2:00 a.m., we were each only on our second scrapbook.

Declan dropped his head back against the couch, rubbing his eyes. "I'm going blind from the small print."

"And trying to figure out smudged words."

"Probably smeared by little kids' hands that were madly clipping and pasting notices into the scrapbook so they could go play with their friends."

"And every other notice includes a Byrne. Were they family, friends, or merely strangers with the same last name? How do we even begin to determine their relationship to Tara's family?"

"And these articles on prize-winning cattle at ploughing events, a mining accident, and such. Were they about family or just local news that Tara's great-granny sent her daughter after she moved to Donegal? I'm wrecked. Time for bed." Declan leaned over and placed a warm kiss against my neck, then trailed his lips up to my chin, teasing my mouth.

The research could wait.

Staring into my eyes, he gently laid me back against the couch. Things were about to get hot and heavy...on Emily's couch. As if reading my mind, Declan led me from the room, closing the door behind us to keep out Mac. My sleeping dog wasn't going to be happy when I kicked him out of our bed.

This was one battle with Mac I would win.

CHAPTER
FOURTEEN

The following morning, I was in the kitchen singing a happy tune, making tea. A night of mind-blowing sex, rather than sleep, had left me feeling more rested than I had in weeks. Declan's and my relationship was definitely back on track.

Mac trotted over and dropped his bowl at my feet. I filled it with dog food, then stopped shy of setting it on the floor.

Did he have me trained or what?

"Yeah, things are about to change."

The training manual had recommended having the dog on a leash so the owner controlled the situation. I stuck his bowl of food in the cupboard and went out to the foyer to grab his leash off the coatrack. I returned to the kitchen to find Mac scarfing up pieces of dog food scattered across the pea-green linoleum. He'd jumped up and knocked the container off the counter. The plastic lid had popped open upon impact with the floor.

"No! Naughty!" I clapped my hands and did every other thing the training manual advised against.

Declan flew into the kitchen. "Jaysus, what the bloody hell?"

"I'm training Mac!"

The dog was still gobbling up food.

Declan pulled the leash from my clenched hand and hooked it to Mac's collar. "Right, then, how about I be doing the feeding? Ya got a lot going on right now."

I nodded, shaking with anger.

Declan led Mac toward the back door. The dog pulled on the leash, stopping to eat every piece of food he could along the way. Declan finally tugged him out the back door.

After sweeping up the dog food, I made a cup of tea, double bagging it for extra caffeine. I sat at the desk in the peach room, staring out at the flowers perking up the Coffey cottage. Taking a calming breath, I checked e-mail.

Enid had replied that she'd never seen photos of her grandma in her younger days, but the woman in the pic might have her chin. She'd forwarded the snap to her brother Oliver, keeper of their family photo albums. And yes, Eleanora may indeed have gone by Nellie in her youth. Enid had only known her by her proper name.

As usual, not exactly a helpful e-mail.

Luckily, Emily confirmed that James in the photo was her older brother. She'd never heard of Polly, Nellie, or Richard S. Possibly James's college friends from St. Andrew's University. I was familiar with Scotland's oldest university, since Prince William and

Kate, Duchess of Cambridge, had met there. Had Richard S. possibly been Enid's grandma's Scottish visitor that her hubby had kicked out?

The university's website listed graduates by name or term. It didn't take long to review the handful of students who'd graduated from 1908 to 1920. No Richard S. or James Daly. They apparently hadn't finished college. At least not there. It was worth a shot.

I checked Enid's DNA status on the website that compared results from the top three DNA companies. Still processing...

By midafternoon, we were down to three scrapbooks, zero clues. My mind was mush. Our eyes and brains needed a break, so Declan decided to give the gate another coat of paint while I painted the cottage's front door. We'd almost finished when Emily Ryan pulled up in a black car. I joined Declan as he talked to her through the open car window.

"I was visiting my friend Margaret in Mullingar and thought I'd drive past to see all the lovely landscaping Declan had mentioned." She smiled at Grandma's cottage. "So nice to have the Coffey place almost looking lived in once again."

"Come up and see the rest," Declan said.

"I shouldn't. I don't like calling in unannounced, as if I'm checking up on you."

We assured her it was fine. It was her house, after all. Declan opened the gate, and Emily headed up the drive. When we joined her at the house, she was admiring the purple and pink pom-pom bushes.

"These are lovely. It's been decades since anything other than weeds have grown here." She peered at me, a sparkle in her gray eyes. "And I'm so glad you decided to move in here, luv."

Declan slipped an arm around my shoulder. "Me too."

My chest tightened over the thought of having the dreaded talk with Declan. Now wasn't the appropriate time to discuss our living situation, putting Emily in an awkward position.

We stepped inside the house, and Emily sniffed the air. "My, it is smelling fresh as daisies in here, isn't it now? Such a difference in merely a few weeks."

Declan nodded. "Will start painting the inside this week. Any colors you prefer?"

"Something that brightens up the place and makes it homier. My children always referred to the house as a museum. I can understand why. Quite dreary, isn't it?"

The grim portraits lining the hallway didn't help.

Crap. I glanced over at the yellow tea towel covering her grandpa's scary face. Did I ignore it and hope she didn't notice or try to discreetly pull it off while walking past?

Emily followed my gaze. "I always wanted to cover up that painting. Doesn't exactly give visitors a warm greeting, does it now?"

"Sorry. I feel like his eyes are always following me."

She nodded. "Suppose that's why I've never taken the paintings to the house in Dublin."

Sadly, she didn't mention doing so this trip either.

"We should take tea out back," she said. "Such a lovely day."

Ten minutes later we were seated in the backyard, drinking tea, eating biscuits, and admiring my fairy garden. Mac lay next to the path under the fence, keeping watch for his buddy or Stewey.

Omigod. I'd forgotten to feed Stewey. If he'd even returned. I went over and slipped two cookies under the fence. If a mouse could eat chocolate buttons, a rabbit should be able to eat cookies. Declan arched a curious brow, but Emily was staring over the fence at the treetops.

"So how is the research going for that lad Liam?"

"Haven't started. I have to first finish up with another client." I didn't mention nasty Enid was the other client. Emily had already returned to Ireland when Enid had hired me.

"I was thinking I might like to take a look at the house back there." The wrinkles in Emily's forehead deepened. "I can't believe that place is still standing after all these years. My father often mentioned tearing it down. Too bad he hadn't." She placed a hand against her chest, letting out a ragged breath.

"Are you okay?" I asked.

She nodded, setting down her teacup with a shaky hand. "It seems like a lifetime ago. I haven't seen my daughter since that day I discovered they were still in that house. I was so upset she hadn't heeded my warnings to leave, I threatened to contact the garda. Call the garda on my own daughter, can you imagine? We both said some awful things, and she left. Never saw her again. Not even after her man was killed in the bombing. That was over thirty years ago."

The bombing that had killed Liam's father?

"The young lad in your snaps looks much like my daughter, Noreen." Emily's eyes watered.

As if on cue, Mac trotted over to her with the missing lace doily hanging from his mouth. Where had he been hiding that? Of course, he picked now to return it. Yet it was also a proud mommy moment. He was compassionate enough to realize Emily needed a hanky to wipe her tears.

Emily took the soiled doily without questioning why Mac had the vintage piece of lace.

"The saddest part is I was most upset about the hideout because my father would have disapproved, especially since her gentleman friend was Catholic. How silly was that? Allowing my father to still influence my beliefs from his grave. And I turned out just like him. Estranged from my child."

Undoubtedly why her father's portrait was also hanging in the hallway rather than at her home in Dublin.

Emily wiped away a tear before it trailed down her flushed cheek.

I placed a hand gently on hers. "I'm so sorry. But you don't have to be estranged from your grandson. I know he'd want to meet you. I have his e-mail and phone number."

A look of hope brightened the woman's somber mood. "What would I say to him?"

"Everything you wished you could have said over the past thirty years but were unable to." I texted Liam's contact info to Emily.

Surely Liam would be anxious to meet his grandmother and I hadn't gotten Emily's hopes up for nothing. I had a good track record for bringing people together. I was even doing a better job with Declan and me.

Late that evening, I was relaxing on a lounge chair under an outdoor light in the fairy garden, reading the last scrapbook through blurry eyes. Declan and Mac had gone to bed hours ago. I took a sip of tea, enjoying the quiet evening without annoying mosquitos buzzing around. My dad always referred to the insect as Wisconsin's state bird. I wanted to rest my eyes but was afraid I'd fall asleep if I closed them. Another reason I was sitting outside. The fresh air was keeping me awake.

I came across an obit for a Grainne Byrne, who died in Arklow, County Wicklow. The name jumped out at me because I'd never heard it until Tara mentioned her aunt Grainne. It would make sense that Tara's grandpa William named a daughter after his mother based on the Irish family naming pattern. The woman had died in 1938 at the age of fifty-seven. She'd fit the estimated age of Tara's great-grandma.

This Grainne had eight children, including a William, and four siblings that matched the names Tara had given me. The obit also noted that out-of-town guests included Patrick and Mary Cofee. As in Coffey? Were these Grandma's parents or merely a coincidence? A *huge* coincidence?

Grainne Byrne died in Arklow, where my Mary Coffey's Flannery family had lived. Had Grainne and

Mary been childhood friends? Or maybe relatives? The women's possible connections ping-ponged around my head. Could Grainne Byrne have been Mary's sister?

I gasped.

Their brother...Cousin Enid's biological grandpa?

That would mean *I* was related to nasty Cousin Enid!

Heart racing, I sprang from the chair.

Calm down. Stop thinking the worst-case scenario!

First off, I didn't know if this was my Patrick and Mary Coffey. Second, even if they were, maybe they'd merely been Grainne Byrne's friends. Third, was this Grainne even Tara's great-grandma? Fourth, did I *want* to know the answers to these questions?

I pressed a palm against my forehead, my mind scrambling for how to proceed.

I searched Enid's DNA matches for Flannery connections. There were two, without family trees. With thirty thousand DNA matches, there were bound to be connections to every Irish surname.

I needed to find out this Grainne's maiden name, which wasn't mentioned in the obituary. I was lucky it had given her first name and not merely referred to her as Mrs. Francis Byrne.

Byrne was a common name. Had Grainne been a common one at that time? The church and civil marriage records would have noted her maiden name. I wasn't sure about a death certificate. Her name should also be on her children's baptismal records. I knew from researching Grandma that the County Wicklow records were only online until 1900. Based on Grainne's age, she'd likely had kids at the times of the

1901 and 1911 censuses. Knowing the names and ages of those born before 1900 would enable me to search for baptismal records.

I took a sip of tea, hands trembling from too much caffeine and anxiety. I stared at the cup.

Had I been drinking out of a Flannery's china cup at Tara's? I should have checked the bottom of the cup. I was always on the lookout for Flannery china. It was too late to call her.

I searched Ireland's 1901 census. Only one Grainne Byrne was listed in Wicklow with her husband and two children, birthplace County Westmeath. I slid my gaze in the direction of my Coffey cottage, goose bumps skittering across my skin. I searched for the baptismal records of her two children born before 1900 and finally found one with a mother, Grainne *Coffey*.

My stomach dropped.

Just because she'd been a Coffey born in Westmeath didn't mean she was my great-grandpa Patrick's sister. She could have been a distant rellie. I needed to trace my Coffey tree back to determine Patrick's siblings' names. To prove that Enid *wasn't* descended from Patrick and Grainne's brother!

What about that Richard S. guy in the photo? And the Scottish one who'd visited Enid's grandma and her husband had kicked him out? They were still possibilities? Right?

I headed inside in serious need of Taytos and caffeine. After midnight, yet I still had a long night ahead of me.

Two hours later, I tossed an empty Taytos bag on the cocktail table along with a half dozen others, ready to hit Declan's whiskey.

I'd connected Grainne Coffey Byrne to my Patrick Coffey.

Rather than being Patrick's sister-in-law, they'd been siblings, along with six brothers, two sisters, and however many more I hadn't found birth records for. My head was ready to explode with names and dates. I frantically typed the info into my family tree.

How did I determine if their brother was Enid's biological grandfather? That Enid, Tara's mom, and my mom shared great-grandparents?

Declan entered the room, wearing a lazy smile and a pair of blue flannel pajama bottoms resting low on his waist, no top. Even his half-naked bod couldn't get me to stop typing away on my computer.

"It's almost four. Ya must be wrecked." He raked a hand through his mussed-up hair. "Find a good clue, did ya?"

I shook my head. "It's an awful clue. I might be related to Cousin Enid."

Declan's tired eyes widened. "Jaysus, ya must be delusional from exhaustion."

"I wish."

I rattled off everything I'd discovered.

"True or not, ya have to be getting some sleep or you're gonna have a breakdown."

"My breakdown happened three hours ago when I discovered I'm likely related to Enid." I grabbed my teacup.

Declan wrapped his hand around mine, lowering the teacup from my mouth, slipping it from my hand. "You're shaking something fierce. If ya don't have a heart attack from discovering you're related to Enid, you'll have one from ODing on caffeine." He set the cup on the table. "Take a sleeping pill and get some rest. Go at it again with a clear head in the morning."

"I'm not going to bed unless you promise me I'll wake up and realize this was all a nightmare."

Declan frowned, unable to make me any guarantees. Like he always said, when it came to family, you took the good with the shite. Enid was definitely shite!

"You'll need to be in good form when approaching Enid with the fact that she's descended from a poor Irish land tenant rather than a prestigious English family."

"I need more evidence before I can approach her."

I needed to confront Enid with my ducks in a row.

And a fair amount of booze in my bloodstream.

CHAPTER FIFTEEN

Despite popping a sleeping med, I'd only slept three hours before waking up to a squawking hen. Like it or not, that thing was learning to fend for itself. I slipped jeans on over my plaid leggings for extra protection from the bird's claws and Declan's long-sleeved Guinness T-shirt over my head. I trudged downstairs and pulled on my purple wellies. I grabbed the disgusting chicken treats and gardening gloves from the kitchen counter. Declan had taped a note to the cupboard that he and Mac had run out to grab a few groceries.

I went down and peeked in the cottage's window to find the hen perched on the brick. Plucking a treat from the bag wasn't easy while wearing gloves. I tossed a dried worm onto the dirt floor near the door. The chicken devoured it and peered expectantly at me. I tossed one under the window. It snatched it up in midair. Neat trick. It scratched at the floor for another one.

"Let's get this straight. I'm training *you*, not the other way around."

I threw a treat in the air outside the window. The hen flew out of the house and searched the ground for the worm.

"Yay! See how easy that was? What you can do if you're motivated and put your mind to it? Perseverance."

When the bird failed to find the treat, it eyed the bag in my hand.

"Don't even think of it."

The hen flew at me.

I dodged it. Once again losing at a game of chicken.

Rather than giving in and tossing the package of treats at the bird, I took off running out the gate. The chicken could only fly twenty feet before having to land and then run several feet before taking flight again. I was leading the bird home, a half mile away, to tell the owner to control her poultry. I rounded the bend, startling an elderly man in a neon-yellow vest walking his dog. An oncoming car slowed down, as did two cars behind it. The last one was Declan, shaking his head at me as I ran past. Mac's bark followed me down the road.

I was losing steam, and the chicken was gaining on me by the time I reached its home. The owner was in the yard, gardening. I tossed the package of worms over the chicken-wire fence. The hen joined the others fighting for the treats.

I circled around past the woman, trying to catch my breath. "You need a higher fence!"

I glanced over my shoulder. Coast clear, I stopped running, gasping for air. By the time I reached Emily's, my heart rate was nearly back to normal. I was feeling invigorated. Ready to embark on my genealogy research and to prove Enid and I weren't related.

Declan was in the kitchen unpacking groceries while Mac ate. He smirked, a playful glint in his blue eyes.

"I don't want to hear it." I snagged a bag of Taytos off the counter. "That's the last time I'm trying to help a chicken."

An hour later I'd polished off three bags of chips and was in the peach room working on my Coffey tree. I'd located three of my Patrick's siblings and their descendants in Ireland. The other ones had no paper trail that I could find. I needed to compare my tree to Rosie's with five thousand names. I'd e-mailed her two days ago. Was it too stalkerish to follow up?

Declan entered the room. "Ya need to be taking a break from the computer."

I shook my head. "What if I get a message?"

"Ya have internet on your mobile."

"But I don't have an Ancestry.com app."

"Grand. Won't be needing one to pick out paint colors. Will only take an hour."

After whining for several minutes, I showered and got dressed. We were off to buy paint.

While riding in the car, I texted Zoe.

How are things with Carrig?

Going on a proper date tonight. With my track record that will likely be the end of it. Will be a spinster like my auntie Maeve.

Good luck...

The paint aisle at the home improvement center was shorter, yet more overwhelming, than the cereal aisle at my old store. Ireland's grocery stores were much smaller than in the US, making it easier to stay focused, allowing quicker shopping trips. But all these paint shades looked similar.

My mind was a blur.

I perused the yellows, honing in on a familiar shade. "Light Primrose reminds me of my grandma's kitchen."

Declan put two cans of the paint in our cart.

"How about Warm Parchment for the foyer and hallway?" The light creamy beige tone was similar to Grandma's living room.

"Grand for the kitchen cupboards also."

"And lavender for our bedroom." The color of her apron I used to wear while helping her bake cookies.

It would kill old man Daly to know that his house would be painted in Grandma's favorite colors.

Declan brushed a kiss to my lips. "*Our* bedroom. I love the sound of that."

So did I...

My phone dinged in my purse. An e-mail from Tara. She'd discovered that Rosie's family tree was no longer private. For some reason it wasn't linked to her profile.

"Let's start with this paint and come back for the rest."

A half hour later, I sat at the desk in the peach room, searching Rosie's tree. Her grandfather was Hugh Coffey, born in Westmeath. No siblings listed. My Patrick had a brother Hugh I hadn't located. I clicked on this Hugh's naturalization papers. He'd immigrated to America from Killybog, Westmeath, in 1910.

The year Enid's dad, Edward Daly, was born.

Had he fled Ireland to avoid responsibility? Had his family disowned him for getting an English girl pregnant? A friend of their enemy Daly family to boot? That might have caused the family's rift more so than the English landlord versus Irish tenant or Catholic versus Protestant conflicts. Had Enid's supposed grandpa married her grandma knowing she was pregnant? To save her honor, or had he loved her?

Even though Rosie and Enid shared a grandpa, Hugh Coffey, they didn't share much more DNA than they did with Tara's mom, who shared their *great*-grandparents. That proved just how difficult it was to pinpoint the relationship of a connection and that everyone inherited different amounts of their ancestors' DNA.

I pulled up the attached 1940 US Census record. Hugh had lived in a small New York town with his wife, daughter, and Bridget Daly. After months of wondering where Grandma had lived for the nine years between arriving in America and marrying Grandpa Brunetti in Wisconsin, it made me happy to learn she hadn't been alone after emigrating. She'd lived with family.

Even though that family was related to Enid!

I joined Declan in the hallway where he was rolling primer onto the dark-green walls, prepping them for a light creamy parchment color. I shared my findings. That Tara's mom, Enid, Rosie, and my mom shared great-grandparents.

I collapsed back against the staircase railing. "Who's going to take this news worse? My family or Cousin Enid? Or poor George. Finding out he's related to her but through the Coffeys, not the Dalys, will definitely take the bounce out of his step. Yet I can't disclose anything without Enid's approval. Good thing. If Rachel was pissed about me taking Enid on as a client, she'd flip out over this."

"Maybe you'll be able to keep it a secret."

"Wish I could keep it a secret from Enid. Unfortunately, she paid me to do a job."

"And ya did a damn good one."

I nodded. "Too good."

Once Enid learned the truth, she'd refuse to pay me. Precisely why I'd send her an invoice requiring cash payment before handing over the research. Of course, I'd only charge her for half my time, or she'd dispute the bill. She'd never believe yesterday had been a twenty-hour day. And I'd bill her for our round-trip mileage to Donegal, not merely gas money.

Even if I shared my discovery for free, she wasn't going to be happy with the bomb I was about to drop.

I certainly wasn't.

CHAPTER SIXTEEN

I'd felt like puking my guts out the entire ferry ride across the Irish Sea. Now I knew how poor Mac had felt on his first trip to England. No way could Enid take the news of her, or rather *our*, family tree worse than I was. Except that she now had a poor Irish land tenant's blood running through her veins rather than that of a wealthy English estate owner. Her grandpa had abandoned her unwed grandmother. Her father had been conceived out of wedlock. The bright side was her grandpa Daly had been an upstanding guy, raising another man's child. If he'd even known...

Declan offered to go with me to Enid's, afraid of her reaction. I'd insisted he stay at George's. I needed to do this myself. *How* I was going to do it, I hadn't a clue.

Enid lived in a modest-sized stone cottage with a thatched roof. Ivy climbed up the house and wrapped around the windows. Colorful flowers bordered a cobblestone path leading to a green front door. It resembled a fairy-tale cottage. Yet there were plenty of wicked witches in fairy tales.

I rang the doorbell.

"Ding Dong! The Witch Is Dead" played in my head.

She wasn't. I could hear footsteps and a dog yipping on the other side of the door. Enid appeared in casual tan slacks, flats, and a white blouse. The first time I'd seen her out of riding attire. She held the cutest dog ever, besides Mac. He was small and black with white patches. I couldn't believe Enid had a dog after she'd called Mac a horrible creature on more than one occasion and threatened him harm. I also couldn't believe the dog seemed to like her.

I stepped into the foyer, painted a sage green with white furnishings. Enid closed the door. She set the dog gently on the wooden floor, and he sniffed my leg. Worried that she'd trained him to pee on me, I moved my leg and gave him a pat.

Enid shooed him away from me. "Now run along, Charlie."

Charlie. Enid's Ancestry profile name.

She led me into a sitting room painted a lighter green with a yellow floral-patterned couch and chairs. Riding trophies, ribbons, and photos of Enid throughout the years filled a credenza. A painting of a younger Enid on a black horse hung over the marble fireplace. Did she still ride? No stables were out back, and no horse was in the surrounding fields.

"This is a business call, not a social one, so I don't have any biscuits or scones. Would you care for a spot of tea?"

"Do you have something stronger?"

"Sherry."

"Perfect." I'd never tried sherry. Even if it tasted like lighter fluid, it was better than being sober for our conversation. Apparently she felt the same way, returning with two glasses of sherry.

I took a drink for courage. The sweet nutty-flavored wine made my lips purse. I took another swig.

We sat at a table in front of a set of French doors with a lovely view of a colorful garden.

"So what do you have for me?" she asked.

"Did you receive my invoice?" I gazed expectantly at her.

She handed over an envelope.

I opened it.

She rolled her eyes.

Seriously? After she'd shorted me money the last time? I'd already given her an incredible deal on my hours. I wasn't getting screwed. I counted it. One thousand and fifty pounds. The money would pay for my genealogy class this fall. I stuffed it into my purse for safekeeping. I connected my laptop to my phone's hotspot. I removed the materials from the large envelope, hoping the visual aids would help me relax. They'd done the trick in nasty Mrs. Arnold's speech class.

I recounted every detail, starting with my trip to Donegal. The scrapbooks and boxes. Grainne Byrne's obit. I ended with a bang that Enid's DNA matched with Hugh Coffey's line, and mine.

The woman took a sip of sherry, staring expressionless at the table. "What a load of old rot." She slid her gray-eyed gaze to mine. "What about that one Joyce DNA match who's related to James Joyce?"

So *that* was why she'd agreed to me conducting the research. If she couldn't be a Daly, she could be a descendant of Ireland's famous writer.

"He might be a distant relation, but I'm telling you, Hugh Coffey was your grandfather, not Albert Daly."

Her gaze sharpened. "You fabricated this entire research. A scam for revenge and to cheat me out of my money."

"I wouldn't make up being related to you for a million bucks. It certainly wasn't worth the fourteen hundred pounds you paid me."

"Which you shall return." She held out her hand.

"I'm not giving you back your money."

"Then I'll sue for it."

"Go ahead. All I have to do is take a DNA test to prove we're related." My stomach tossed at the thought.

"As if I'm leaving my results on that site."

I took a screenshot of Enid's account and top DNA matches.

"What'd you just do?"

"Nothing."

As if an account in the name of Charlie proved anything. I quickly clicked over to her profile page with her e-mail address and personal info.

Enid sprang to her feet. "What are you doing?"

I popped up from my chair, scrambling to take a screenshot while racing toward the front door like the fired employee at the Kerry meeting. Enid was hot on my heels.

"A court can call your DNA into evidence," I yelled over my shoulder as I raced out the door. "Would you want this to go public?"

An earth-shattering slam filled the air and vibrated through my chest.

Was that a no?

☙ ❧

I paced in the garden alongside George's house. My body trembled with anger while I filled Declan in on my confrontation with Enid. "Just when I thought nothing could be worse than being related to that wretched woman, she threatens to sue me. As if she can sue me because I discovered we're related!"

"Did you say we're related to Cousin Enid?" Rachel flew around the front corner of the house. "She's *our* cousin?"

I nodded reluctantly.

"What the hell, Caity? How did that happen?" The vein in the middle of my sister's forehead pulsated. Something I hadn't seen happen in months. "You need to double-check your research. I told you not to take her on as a client!"

"As if I ever dreamed I'd find out we're related."

Enid appeared, her top lip curled into a sneer.

Shit. I'd been so upset I hadn't locked the gate.

"What do you want?" Declan demanded.

Enid glared at me. "I came to collect the documents which I paid for and you took. It seems I have an even better case against you now that you breached the confidentiality agreement."

I snagged the envelope off the table and thrust it at Enid.

Rachel grabbed my arm. "What are you doing?"

"She paid for it."

Enid snatched the envelope from my hand. "I'll be contacting every genealogical society in Ireland to ensure you are blacklisted. Not to mention the Better Business Bureau." She spun around and clomped off.

Rachel flew after her.

I ran in front of my sister. "Don't make things worse."

"How can they be worse unless Enid is our mother?"

We both missed a beat even though we knew that wasn't possible. Yet right now anything seemed possible if we were related to horrible Cousin Enid!

"Even if she doesn't sue me for breach of privacy, Ireland's Better Business Bureau will shut me down just when I'm finally getting started."

"Was telling her the truth worth the money?" Rachel demanded.

"I had to tell her. Even if it wasn't worth fourteen hundred pounds."

"I gave her three thousand!" Fanny appeared from around the back of the house, her porcelain skin turning a flaming red.

"You gave her *what*?" I said.

"Money to hire you. To keep the peace before my wedding, and you needed work. George won't allow me to pay for anything. I need to feel like I'm contributing to this family. You're going to be my family also."

"So I took *your* money, not *Enid's*?"

My head was going to explode.

Fanny wilted onto a wooden bench. "Everything is falling apart. Mary broke her arm, so she can't attend the hen party. Evelyn's husband says the parties are too risqué and won't *permit* her to attend. So cancel the party. My dress just arrived. It's *purple* rather than *blue*. And now this..." She fanned herself with a blue hanky.

I reined in my anger, afraid Fanny was going to have a stroke. "That was really sweet of you paying Enid, but please don't tell George. If he confronts her, she'll have even more ammunition to come after me."

Rachel placed a comforting hand on Fanny's shoulder. "I'll contact the shop and have your dress taken care of."

"And we'll have the hen party with or without Mary and Evelyn. It's going to be great."

Depending on what Mom had planned.

Fanny nodded, pushing herself up from the bench. "I'm sorry. I'm just a bit stressed. I'll go bake scones for this evening. Baking always makes me feel better."

Sunnyvale's highly anticipated episode aired in three hours. We'd finally know how it was going to impact our futures. I was losing my business just when the estate was taking off. If by chance Lawrence got ditched, I'd be helping Rachel secure new business. My sister would never fire me or allow me to quit. I was a planner for life.

"She won't sue ya," Declan said. "Wouldn't want the public humiliation."

"Enid contacting the genealogical societies will be as bad as being sued. And I betrayed my client's privacy. I violated my work ethics."

"You didn't break the agreement," Declan said. "Rachel overheard it."

"I shouldn't have been discussing it in the open so anyone could hear."

I couldn't believe I agreed with Cousin Enid.

Rachel dropped her head back, letting out an irritated groan. "I'm going to try hard to forget this entire nightmare. But we'll figure out how to handle Enid. In the meantime, you can help full time with the events and move to England for the summer if you want."

Declan shook his head. "She won't be moving here after finally moving into Emily's with me."

Rachel's eyes widened with surprise. "I didn't know you'd moved into Emily's."

I shrugged, my stomach knotting. "Sort of." I couldn't lie. Rachel lived with my landlord.

Declan's gaze sharpened. "Sort of?"

Rachel shot me an apologetic look and slipped away.

"Well, I'm living between Emily's and Dublin."

"When the hell did you decide this?" he demanded.

"I never exactly said that I was giving up my apartment. I'd planned on attending classes, lectures, and genealogy meetings this fall."

"Ever heard of a train to Dublin?" Declan raked a frustrated hand through his hair. "Feckin' unbelievable, Caity. I'm not just upset you didn't tell me ya weren't staying at Emily's but the fact that ya had no plans to actually move in."

"What about you looking at the Whelan place? If you'd moved there and I'd given up my apartment, what would I have done?"

His anger evaporated into disbelief. "Ya think I'd have just up and left ya like that? That's how little ya think of me, of our relationship, is it?"

"What was I supposed to think?"

"Maybe ya should have *asked* me 'bout the Whelan place." He stalked off before I could.

I now wanted to live at Emily's something fierce.

The thought of not staying with Declan at Emily's brought tears to my eyes. Of not waking up by Declan, and Grandma's cottage. Not working together on landscaping and home improvements. No more genealogy super sleuthing with him. He was the Watson to my Sherlock Holmes. My detective partner, confidant, best friend...my everything.

What the hell had I been thinking putting my career before Declan?

CHAPTER
SEVENTEEN

"I can't believe that's our house." George smiled at the TV, where Caroline was preparing to walk down the aisle in the estate's salon. "It looks so different. I guess they say the television adds five kilos."

We all let out faint laughs, gathered around the library's TV. Rachel and I exchanged nervous glances, anxious for the groom to get hitched not ditched. We wouldn't relax until the couple kissed. An alternate ending could have been filmed on a studio set with a reproduction of the estate's fireplace and Caroline tossing her ring into it.

George chuckled. "Wouldn't know that Mac had just filled the room with the stench of rotting eggs."

Mac's ears twitched at the sound of his name. He remained curled up with his eyes closed in front of the fireplace.

George grimaced, peering over at Rachel. "Sorry. I wasn't supposed to worry you over that."

My sister's nervous gaze darted from the TV to me.

I shrugged. "Sorry."

She shook her head, focusing back on the show, tapping a finger against the computer keyboard on her lap. As soon as the credits rolled, she'd hopefully be clicking the Publish button, and the estate's website events and Facebook ads would go live.

"A nice shot of your painting over the fireplace," George told Declan.

Declan nodded, sitting across from me in a chair and not next to me on the couch. We hadn't spoken since our argument in the garden. I should have told him earlier I wasn't moving into Emily's. The fear of losing him was why I hadn't. *That* was what I should have told him. That I *needed* to tell him. Rather than having tried to turn the argument around and make it about the Whelan place.

Fanny sat perched on the edge of the couch, nibbling a scone, which she hoped all of England would soon be eating.

Thomas massaged a hand over his stubbly chin. "I should have added Achillea..."

"The flowers couldn't be lovelier." George gave his friend a reassuring pat on the back. "To think that three months ago I'd been against opening the house to the public, and now here it is for all the world to see. And to appreciate your gardening talents. Wish I'd have agreed to it sooner."

Thomas's worried expression relaxed. "We've come a long way together, haven't we?"

George nodded. "We certainly have, my friend. I appreciate your and everyone's patience with me."

Fanny smiled at my uncle, placing a hand on his.

Even though Enid had flushed my genealogy business down the loo, I'd be able to help George and the estate get out of debt and back on track. *Remain optimistic.*

I peered over at Thomas. "Gardening magazines will be beating down your door to get a spread."

Everyone nodded in agreement.

Thomas sprang from the chair. "I have pruning to do." He flew from the room in his green wellies.

"I bet the high-tea events sell out in an hour," I told Rachel. "And weddings are booked for five years."

Looking overwhelmed, she polished off her glass of wine from a high-end bottle in George's collection.

Caroline and Lawrence kissed in front of the salon's fireplace, sealing their vows, the episode's ending, and our futures!

Rachel and I heaved relieved sighs.

She typed a few keystrokes, and the estate's events were live. She blew out a ragged breath. "Let the games begin."

George placed a loving hand on Fanny's arm. "Is something wrong, dear? You haven't spoken a word since the show began."

Fanny expelled a burst of air through her lips. "Enid is your cousin on the Coffey side, not the Dalys'." She collapsed back against her blue velvet couch.

What happened to Fanny's belief that keeping secrets was good for a relationship?

George's gaze narrowed. "What are you talking about?"

I confessed my discovery.

My uncle frowned, and his shoulders dropped. "Are you quite certain?"

"Ninety-nine percent. I'm going to take a DNA test."

"She can't sue you because you discovered you're related. You have proof it's not a scam. That's the final straw." George surged from the couch. "I'm going over there right—"

"You can't." I flew to my feet. "Don't give her more ammunition against me. She's suing because I violated the confidentiality agreement. Even worse, she's contacting the genealogy societies and the Better Business Bureau. My business is ending before it even began."

"So you have nothing to lose with me going over there."

"Please don't."

"Very well. Give me a moment." He left and returned with an envelope. He handed it to me.

I opened it to find Enid's bogus threat to sue that past spring forged on a solicitor's letterhead. The white paper was wrinkled from me crumpling it in anger and smeared with dirt from Mac's attempt at burying it.

"If I didn't sue Enid over that scandal, she will certainly not be suing you. This woman needs to be stopped. I'll not allow her threats and bullying to continue. If you won't permit me to tell her so, then you must."

I peered at the letter. My golden ticket. My get-out-of-jail-free card. "I don't know." A part of me wanted to shove the letter in Enid's face, yet another part couldn't get over the fact that I'd disclosed her information, even if it had been accidental.

"What's there to know?" Declan's gaze narrowed on me. "Save your job. Commit to something, Caity." His disappointed tone made my stomach drop. He walked out, and Mac followed, taking his father's side.

Everyone gazed off into space as if not having noticed the tension between Declan and me.

I attempted to shove aside Declan's harsh but valid remarks and the icky feeling in my stomach. "Blackmailing Enid would make me no better than her."

"You'd have to take food from the hungry and beds from the homeless to bring yourself down to her level," George said. "There is no comparison."

"What if it had been a different client than Enid?" I asked.

"A different client wouldn't have freaked out over being related to us," Rachel said.

"The person could still have disputed my findings. I understand Enid's anger over discovering she's not a Daly and then to learn her grandfather was Irish when her grandmother had likely loathed the Irish for that exact reason. If I breached someone else's privacy, would I expect that person to understand? Is Enid really being that unreasonable?"

I was proud of my ability to think rationally when my life was in a downward spiral. Gazes narrowed, everyone seemed to be pondering my speech.

"I'm not saying I like or agree with what she's doing, just that I understand where she's coming from."

Rachel shook her head. "Screw the bitch."

"Take that slag down," Fanny added.

George gave a definitive nod. "May she burn in hell."

So much for being rational.

My life had become a bigger flippin' soap opera than *Sunnyvale*!

⅋❧ ❦⅋

That night I was sitting on the library's red couch by myself, staring at my website, thankful I hadn't put a ton of time into it.

My sister entered the room and sat in the tan brocade chair next to the couch. "It would have been more unethical to have not told Enid the truth than having accidentally let me overhear it. I wouldn't have told her the truth."

"I'm sure—"

Rachel held up a hand. "Don't even say that I would have told her because you know I wouldn't have. I also violated the *Sunnyvale* confidentiality clause by telling Gerry about the filming. The show certainly has much better lawyers than Enid. And if lawyers learn she forged a legal document on a solicitor's letterhead, nobody will represent her."

I'd always looked up to Rachel and admired her business sense. But she was right. I had stronger work ethics despite having opened my yap about Enid.

"Don't let Enid bully you. Certainly don't let her keep Fanny's money."

I nodded faintly. Getting Fanny's money back was a priority. If I didn't, I had to at least return what Enid had given to me.

"Tell your side of the story. Dispute Enid's charges. Prospective clients looking at your website won't know what happened with Enid."

"Unless the Better Business Bureau shuts down my site."

"Remember my story about the motivational speaker climbing Mount Everest?"

I nodded. I'd shared the story with the chicken.

"This is just one step backward. Not the end. The estate's Facebook ads already have thousands of likes and comments. I've received two requests for weddings. You deserve the credit for getting us all on board and the estate out of debt. You convinced everyone to do the art-mystery event despite the odds. If it wasn't for that event, Robert Daly wouldn't have wandered in here that day and chosen the estate for the wedding episode, changing our lives. So don't give up now."

Feeling a bit more optimistic, I said, "I'm going to see Enid tomorrow. To get Fanny's money back and try to reason with her."

Rachel shook her head. "You're a bigger person than me. Than any of us. We'd all blackmail the hell out of her. Good luck reasoning with that irrational...woman. Make sure you have a plan B." She headed toward the doorway, then paused and turned. "I'm really proud of you, Caity." She smiled and walked out.

A warm feeling washed over me, and I relaxed back against the couch. Nine months ago Rachel and I had acted more like coworkers than sisters. Our relationship hadn't been a whole lot better than mine and Gemma's. We'd come a long way. And for every step backward we took, I'd make sure we continued moving forward.

Rachel was right. I needed a plan B. If reasoning didn't work and I refused to blackmail Enid, how was I going to get Fanny's money back? Not pursuing legal action over Enid's bogus threat apparently made her think we'd take whatever she handed out. She'd continue bullying us if I didn't stop her.

I had nothing to lose at this point, but Enid had her reputation and status within the community. What if I threatened her with the truth? All I had to do was show up at one of her society functions and introduce myself as her cousin to get the gossip buzzing. Technically, I wouldn't be disclosing her ancestry background.

I pulled up Rosie's family tree to see what else I could use for ammunition. I read through the attachments, including a handwritten history about Hugh Coffey. Before moving to America, the man had belonged to the Irish Republican Brotherhood—a secret fraternal organization dedicated to establishing an independent democratic republic. He'd fled Ireland because he was a wanted man, not because he'd gotten Enid's grandma, Nellie, pregnant. It wouldn't have been safe for her and their unborn son to have been associated with him. He'd returned to Ireland in the spring of 1916 and participated in the famous Easter Uprising, which contributed to an increase in popular support for Irish independence.

Hugh Coffey had been a hero.

At least in the eyes of those Irish seeking independence. Certainly not in the eyes of Enid's English grandma's family, who'd likely felt he'd abandoned her unwed grandma and then added salt to the wound by fighting against their country.

Yet a sense of pride rose inside me.

Enid wouldn't share that feeling even though she shared Hugh Coffey's DNA. She also wouldn't want me sharing the information with her hoity-toity friends. I wouldn't, of course.

But she wouldn't know that.

CHAPTER EIGHTEEN

Rather than waking up next to Declan's warm body and the scent of his woodsy cologne, I woke up in an empty bed, cold cotton sheets against my skin. A pile of blankets lay on the chair where Declan had slept. I almost burst into tears.

Mac barked outside in the distance, followed by Thomas yelling. Great. Had my dog trampled Thomas's prize-winning flowers or peed in the fountain again?

I flew out of bed in my Coffey T-shirt and plaid leggings. I ran down the stairs to find everyone outside in their robes and jammies, watching Mac chase two women around the sprawling lawn. Thomas was supervising the fiasco. One woman snapped pics of the house with her cell phone as she raced toward the front gate.

Rachel wore a huge grin and George's navy velour robe. "How awesome is this? *Sunnyvale* fans scaled the fence."

Fanny smoothed a hand over her white hair and pinched color into her pale cheeks. She tightened the sash on her blue satin robe with a marabou collar. "You never know where the paparazzi might be lurking." She snatched the breathing strip from George's nose.

George massaged the bridge of his nose. "Precisely why I must have the grounds' security system repaired." He peered over at Rachel. "Is that in the estate's budget?"

She nodded. "We could secure Fort Knox with what we'll make from all the events. I've received dozens of e-mails inquiring about wedding bookings, and two high teas have sold out."

Fanny smiled. "I've sold twenty-three packages of scones. Several magazines and a gardening show have contacted Thomas."

Even Mac had benefited from the TV show, back in his element chasing trespassers from the property.

"I'm going to call the security company." George headed inside with Fanny.

"What about Declan's paintings?" I asked Rachel. "Did he sell any?"

"Two of the woman at the desk writing a letter."

My favorite one. "Brilliant."

Speaking of Declan, where was his car?

"Where'd Declan go?"

Rachel's smile faded. "He left fifteen minutes ago."

On his way back to Ireland, no doubt.

Rachel gave me a hug. "I'm sorry. I'm sure you don't feel like celebrating, but this success is all thanks to you. Two months of events and your student loans will be paid off."

"That won't pay off my loans."

"A bonus will. You should be debt-free same as the estate."

Being debt-free was what I'd been working so hard to achieve since escaping my ex. I'd equated standing on my own with financial independence, worried I'd end up on my parents' couch again. My determination to be self-sufficient had pushed Declan away.

I'd rather be in debt for life and with Declan.

≈❧ ❧≈

I skipped showering and got dressed, wanting to get my confrontation with Enid over with. My stomach knotted as I headed up her cobblestone walk holding the paper detailing Hugh Coffey's heroic past in my sweaty hand.

Declan flew out the front door, radiating anger. He came to an abrupt halt, just feet in front of me. His gaze softened slightly, but his face didn't light up like it usually did upon seeing me.

My heart pounded. "What are you doing here? Did you threaten her with the letter?"

"I threatened her with the truth. Or rather a version of the truth. Told her that Rachel overheard *me* discussing her family tree, not *you*, and you'd merely intervened. You signed the confidentiality agreement. I didn't."

Why hadn't I thought of that?

"What'd she say?"

"Didn't believe me."

Screw Enid. It was a good sign that Declan had come here in my defense. At least he still cared enough to protect me.

"Thanks for trying. I appreciate it."

He nodded faintly.

"I'm so sorry for not being up front about living at Emily's. I'd planned to tell you, but after I learned about the Whelan place, I didn't know what to do. I wanted so badly to make things right again."

Declan's gaze narrowed. "Who told you 'bout that?"

"Mags. But she hadn't realized it was a secret."

"I was looking at it for *us*, not for *me*. A few months ago. When I thought..." He glanced away.

"When you thought what?"

"That once ya got citizenship and knew you'd be staying in Ireland that you'd be wanting to stay with *me*. That we could find a house to make our home. Like the Whelan place."

"Of course, I wanted to stay with you. I still want to stay with you. How could you think I didn't?"

He gave me a bewildered look. "Jaysus, I don't know, Caity."

"Wanting to keep my flat, to pay the rent, to prove to myself I could do it was about me, not about you."

"Loads of this was 'bout *you*."

"I know I was selfish."

"You're so worried about being disrespected. What about disrespecting me? I stayed in that tiny flat for three months to be with you. I couldn't paint or do a thing. When I tried to discuss a larger place, ya shut me down. When I took the caretaker job, ya got pissed. You're so worried about getting into another controlling relationship. Just make sure you aren't the one doing the controlling."

My stomach clenched.

Was he comparing *me* to Andy?

"After looking at Whelan's, I realized it was gonna be a while before ya wanted to live together forever."

Forever?

Before I could compose a coherent response, he heaved a sigh and walked past me down the path. I wanted to run after him, but I feared I'd say something to make things worse.

Could they get worse?

He pulled out of the driveway.

I spun around, glaring at Enid's house. She was at least partially to blame for this fiasco. I pounded on the wooden door. Boots clomped down the hallway on the other side of the door, followed by Charlie yipping. Yet Enid didn't answer. She'd likely peered through the peephole and decided against it.

"Enid, I know you're there."

The door opened a crack, revealing Enid's beady gray eyes and pursed lips. "If you're here to ask me not to pursue the matter, it's too late."

My stomach dropped.

Whom had she contacted?

My fingers curled around the folded paper in my hand, crumpling it.

She eyed the paper. "What's that?" She opened the door wider to snatch it from my hand.

Her dog bolted from the house.

"Charlie!" Enid screamed. "Get back here!"

He raced down the walk toward freedom.

Guess Mac wasn't the only untrained dog.

Enid and I flew after him. Despite all the woman's bicycling, she was lagging far behind me. A car zipped past on the narrow road out front.

"Charlie!" Enid's voice filled with panic.

As I neared the road, fear and adrenaline propelled me forward into the air. I tackled Charlie just feet from the road. A car sped past, a flash of black tires spitting pebbles at us. The dog panted underneath me, his heart beating against my chest. Enid raced up. I was paralyzed, afraid if I moved, Charlie would take off again. Enid, however, was frantic, gasping for air, slapping one hand to her chest, the other to her forehead.

"Stay here!" She raced back toward the house.

Surprisingly, Charlie wasn't squirming to escape. Afraid I was squishing the dog, I relaxed against him.

Enid returned with a leash. She reached under my chest and snapped it on to the dog collar. I raised myself up on all fours, releasing my hold on Charlie. Feeling the pain of my tackle in every joint and muscle, I slowly stood. A jeans knee was torn. Pebbles and sand grit were embedded in my bloody elbows and forearms.

I finally determined I had no broken bones. Enid was sitting on the ground, hugging Charlie tightly against her chest, smothering him with kisses. She sobbed, more upset than when she'd confessed she wasn't a Daly.

She peered up at me through a teary gaze. "Thank you. I hadn't"—she choked back a sob—"pursued my threat. And I won't." She continued kissing her dog.

Would she pursue her Coffey connections? Would she one day want to learn about her grandpa, Hugh Coffey? If she did, I'd tell her.

CHAPTER NINETEEN

I lay on my couch, pillows propped behind my back, computer on my lap, Mac at my feet. Mac had gotten out of bed to eat, allowing me to fill his bowl without diving in for the food. Either Declan had done a stellar job training him or Mac was in a funk. After eating, he'd gone back to sleep on the couch. Reruns of the sitcom *Mrs. Brown's Boys* was on TV. Even the lively banter between Mrs. Brown—an older woman played by a male actor—and her neighbor friend Winnie couldn't make us laugh. We were a pathetic pair.

In the past two days, we'd only left the apartment for Mac to go potty at the dog park three blocks away. I needed to walk to the grocery store. I'd reused the last tea bag a half dozen times. The remaining sheets of paper towels were on the bathroom counter next to the toilet. I shook the crumbs from the last bag of Taytos into my mouth.

A text dinged on my phone. I snatched it off the cocktail table, heart racing. It was Zoe, not Declan.

Please tell Rachel I'll have a guest for the wedding.

I smiled for the first time in days. Never in my wildest dreams would I have imagined Zoe and Carrig together. However, double dating probably wasn't in our near future. Declan and I were in limbo, and he was going to flip out when he discovered his sister's new beau.

I replied with a slew of celebratory emojis, then sank back against the couch.

Declan hadn't responded to the text I'd sent yesterday morning. I'd chickened out and texted instead of calling. Even a voicemail would have been more personal than a text. Wanting to discuss our relationship, I hadn't mentioned I was keeping my career as a result of Charlie's rescue. If I hadn't heard from Declan by lunch, I was calling him.

Speaking of Charlie, I'd been so frazzled after saving him from being hit by a car I'd forgotten to demand Fanny's money back. I was halfway to George's when I'd remembered. I'd returned to Enid's, but she hadn't answered the door. Giving her the benefit of the doubt, that she was too distraught for company and not back to her old wretched self, I'd shot her an e-mail.

I still hadn't heard from her.

Determined to get out of my funk, I finished completing the volunteer form for a genealogical society. Participating in a transcription project for marriages found in unusual sources outside of civil registration or church records would help me gain research experience. I'd also become more proficient at reading faded documents with fancy or chicken-scratch handwriting.

A ding signaled the arrival of an e-mail. Liam. Emily

and he were meeting at her Dublin home today. He couldn't thank me enough for connecting him with his grandma. My eyes watered at the thought of what would undoubtedly be a very emotional encounter. What if I hadn't been there that day Liam had knocked on the door? He'd likely have searched for the hideout and left without me having known he was there. Funny how one knock on a door had been a major turning point in Liam's and Emily's lives. And now George had another rellie.

Feeling slightly inspired, I dragged my butt off the couch. Mac didn't open his eyes or go racing for his leash by the door.

"I'm going down to check the mail. You want to come?"

Mac cracked an eyelid, then shut it.

"Enough with the pity party. Come on."

He tucked his face under his paw, covering his eyes.

Fine. I headed down the stairs to the building's entrance. One lone piece of mail sat in the box. A postcard with two sheep in the Scottish Highlands. The word bubble next to the lamb read, *Are you my great-grandpa?* I smiled at Bernice and Gracie's card.

Met up with our third cousin Ian McKinney in the Highlands. Having fun except for the haggis. Thanks so much for making our dreams come true! Tell Mac hi!

Researching Bernice and Gracie's great-grandpa McKinney had been my most difficult project to date. My first clients' confidence in my ability to conduct ancestry research had set me on the path to becoming a genealogist. And if I hadn't met them, I'd never have won Mac. The women had entered me in a contest without my permission while I was escorting a Dublin consumer promotion.

At the time, I'd been a bit miffed. I'd barely been able to take care of myself, let alone a dog. My only pets growing up had been my cat, Izzy, and hamster, Bruno. And besides the financial aspect, Mom wouldn't have been keen on caring for a dog while I was traveling the world. I'd suggested that Bernice and Gracie give Mac to the Irish hotties they'd just met. I couldn't believe I'd done such a thing. Luckily, Declan's parents had graciously taken Mac in. I couldn't imagine my life without him.

I also couldn't imagine my life without Declan.

"Mac, grab your bowl and pack your stuff. We're going to see Daddy. Even if he doesn't want to see us."

❧ ❧

I went down to the pub to ask Gerry if I could borrow his car. He was behind the bar, Rachel seated across from him. Gazes locked, they were oblivious to my arrival.

"I didn't know you were in Ireland," I said.

Rachel glanced over at me. "It wasn't planned. But Gerry couldn't make it over until the weekend. Since our afternoon teas don't start until Friday, I thought I'd plan from here."

Gerry grinned. "And I'll be going back with her to assist. You're looking at your event's busboy and dishwasher." He removed a glass from the sudsy water.

"If there's one thing I'm brilliant at, it's washing dishes."

No pruned fingers was one less thing for me to worry about.

"You're good at more than that." Rachel flashed him a flirty smile. She peered over at me, her smile fading. "Sorry. Shouldn't be acting so lovey-dovey. Have you spoken to Declan?"

I shook my head. "I'm heading to Emily's right now. If Declan doesn't want me to move in there, then I'll live at Grandma's. Will just need to put in some windows, electricity, heat, and a few other luxuries."

"Good for you," Rachel said. "And I'm sorry, again. I never should have brought up your living in England. *I* don't even want to live there full time. I'd just been overwhelmed at the thought of the events exploding and me not being able to handle them. Afraid I wouldn't be able to manage the stress, like at Brecker. I'm also sorry I put so much off on you."

"Yeah, I was freaking out."

"The hype will die down within a month or so. We'll be good."

"Honestly, I hope the events don't die down for a bit. It would be great to have money in the bank for emergencies, like a new roof. So we're not always flying by the seat of our knickers to survive."

The story of my life.

But not for long.

The perky yellow and red flowers bordering Grandma's cottage made my chest tighten. Who'd have thought that domestic chores could have been so much fun and would have brought Declan and me closer together? Or that I'd have grown attached to the Daly home and considered it *my* home? At the sight of Declan's car parked in front of the house, a nervous feeling tossed my tummy. Mac sat in the passenger seat, tail wagging.

"Yeah, I'm excited too." But more nervous.

The dog raced to the door, barking. I rang the doorbell. I hadn't rung Emily's doorbell since Christmastime, when I'd first met her. I'd been a bundle of nerves. Anxious to learn what Emily knew about Grandma and trying to come to terms with Declan and I having just broken up. After meeting Emily and discovering her brother and Grandma's heart-wrenching past, I'd gone down to Grandma's cottage, contemplating my future. Declan had shown up and apologized for being emotionally distant, a survival tactic after losing his wife, Shauna. He'd said *I love you* for the first time. I'd forgiven him rather than walking out the rusted gate like Grandma had eighty years ago, leaving her family behind.

Hopefully, he'd remember the second chance I'd given him and now give me one.

Declan answered the door in flannel jammie bottoms, no shirt.

My breath caught in my throat.

He squinted at the sunshine, raking a hand through his mussed-up hair, looking like he'd just rolled out of bed. He appeared in worse shape than me. A good sign.

He brushed a hand across Mac's back. The dog's tail whipped against Declan's leg.

"Mac wanted to visit."

Declan's hand froze on Mac's back.

"So did I." When he didn't respond, I added, "If that's okay."

He nodded faintly, standing.

Having nothing to lose, I blurted out, "I'm sorry. Trying so hard to be self-reliant made me selfish. I worried too much about falling back into debt, unable to take care of myself. But staying here at Emily's proved that I can stand on my own. Yet I don't want to. I could never be too independent to not need you. I'm sorry it seemed that way."

Declan peered past me, down the drive. "Yeah, it did seem that way."

"After my meeting with Nicholas's friends, I realized how badly I wanted to live here, but I needed to be in Dublin to pursue my career. But when I thought I'd lost you and my career, losing you devastated me way more. I could find another career, but I'll never find another man I love as much as you."

Declan met my gaze, his expression unreadable.

My palms sweated, and I inhaled a shaky breath. "Mac and I want to stay here. Not just for today and tomorrow, but for however long you want to be here."

Declan heaved a sigh. "Caity..."

Panicked by the sound of his sigh, I interjected, "If that's not okay, then I'll live down at my grandma's. Where we first said I love you." Fighting back tears, I turned to walk down the driveway.

Declan grasped my arm, and I turned toward him. His gaze softened. "Of course, I want ya to be living here. And I still love you." He brushed a kiss to my lips.

I threw my arms around his neck and kissed him like we were both going off to battle. He slipped his arms around my waist and pulled me snugly against his bare chest. When we finally came up for air, we stared into each other's eyes, breathing heavily, smiling.

"I promise to never keep anything from you again. At least not about me. But if it's not my secret to tell..." However, Declan would discover Zoe was dating Carrig when he showed up with her at George and Fanny's wedding. I told Declan about their relationship, except for the sex in his parents' driveway part.

His eyes widened in shock, then his expression slowly relaxed. "Nothing is going to spoil my good mood. Not even that wanker. And I promise to never keep things from you unless, of course, it's a present. Even though I'd wanted the Whelan place to be a good surprise, it caused more problems in the end."

Squawking filled the air.

For the love of God. "That thing is back?"

We walked down the drive hand in hand toward the cottage, Mac trotting alongside us. I pushed open the door with more ease than usual. Declan had replaced the rusted hinges.

The hen waddled out, followed by five tiny brownish-yellow chicks racing after their mother. Mac tilted his head to the side, clearly curious about where the others had come from. Appearing less threatened by the little guys, he didn't head for the hills.

"Can't be more than a few days old," Declan said. "Looks like ya couldn't be living here anyway, seeing as the cottage is occupied."

I nodded. "They made Grandma's house a home again."

"So did you." Declan gestured to the flowers and green door.

Rather than waddling off down the road, the hen searched the grass for dried worms. When it didn't find any treats, it swiveled its head in my direction, eying my hand.

"Don't even think about it." The sore on my leg throbbed.

While Declan ran up to the house for treats, the hen went over and ate wild raspberries from a bush. The chicks followed her lead. A white rabbit hopped out of the tall grass and joined them. Stewey! Thank God he was okay.

Declan returned with the treats, scattering them on the ground. He eyed the rabbit. "Stewey, is it?"

I nodded and told him about Mickey's request and the rabbit appearing a few days later. "So we'll need some rabbit food also. And some sort of bed for the baby chicks. And I need to give the hen a name."

Declan quirked a curious brow. "Plan on keeping them, do ya?"

"Not sure we have a choice. I have no clue how to raise chickens. Maybe Mags could be my chicken mentor."

"Sure she could."

"How about Henny Penny for a name?"

"That's grand. Different. But it rhymes."

My gaze narrowed in disbelief. "You've never heard of Henny Penny?"

He shook his head.

"Your mom never read you the fairy tale?"

"Don't think so."

"How about Chicken Little?"

"The one who thought the sky was falling?"

I nodded. "That was another name for it. And her friends Foxy Loxy, Turkey Lurkey, and Goosey Loosey."

Declan laughed. "A Loosey Goosey in a fairy tale?"

"*Goosey Loosey*. I'll have to make sure *I* do the fairy-tale readings to our..." Children. I clamped my teeth down on my lower lip.

Instead of looking freaked out by my presumption that we'd have kids, Declan's lips curled into a pleased smile.

I quickly changed the subject...for now. "I'll have to make sure its owner is okay with this."

"Can't imagine she's not. Probably tired of madly flapping her arms trying to get the yoke back in the pen."

I smiled. "My grandma would approve of the new tenants."

Declan, Mac, the chickens, Stewey, and I were a bit of a nontraditional family. I knew more than anyone that families came in all shapes and sizes and continued to grow.

CHAPTER
TWENTY

George and Fanny sealed their vows with a kiss under the white tent on the estate's lawn. The song "We Are Family" by Sister Sledge began playing. When Fanny hadn't been able to decide on a recessional song, Mom had recommended the disco tune. The 103 guests blew bubbles into the air as Thomas and I walked down the aisle behind the newlyweds. Thomas's date flashed him a sweet smile. A pretty petite woman ten years his junior, she'd interviewed him for a gardening magazine. It appeared that the *Sunnyvale* wedding episode had gained Thomas more than exposure for his lovely gardens and topiary skills.

Mac sat in a blue tutu on Zoe's lap, between Declan and Zoe's date, Carrig—thirtyish with dark hair, in a navy suit rather than his usual jeans and sports jersey. Declan had trained Mac to carry the ring up the aisle in a blue velvet pouch. Another proud mommy moment. And a proud girlfriend moment that Declan had been civil, even friendly, to Carrig.

Declan's steamy gaze swept down the length of my royal-blue satin dress, a sexy little grin on his lips. He looked totally hot in his black suit and blue oxford.

I couldn't wait to rip off his clothes tonight.

Mom and her sisters, Dottie and Teri, were blowing their noses and wiping their eyes. Tears of joy and likely a few sad ones over George not having attended their weddings. All the things they'd missed out on because of Grandma's secret past. Thankfully, I'd uncovered those secrets, and we'd never miss out on another family event.

Gerry's arm was draped around Rachel's relaxed shoulders. She'd relented and hired a planner for the wedding day so she could attend as a guest. The shade of her blue dress with a flirty skirt matched Gerry's shirt. Guests had been asked to wear something blue for the occasion.

Sadie had on a fancy blue hat and white dress. Seamus's blue tweed blazer swallowed up the thin man, who'd ventured from Ireland for the first time. To attend the wedding and also to visit the *Sunnyvale* filming location, even though he'd denied watching the show, like most men. Emily wore a bright smile and a high-collared indigo-colored dress, and her grandson Liam looked handsome in a blue suit.

Not being privy to the dress code, since she hadn't been invited, Enid wore a mint-green dress and proper white heels. She dropped a pink envelope into the card basket at the back of the tent, then escaped down the drive. Apparently, staying for the reception was too bold after she'd crashed the ceremony. Worried about what she'd written on the card, I bolted over to the blue-chiffon-draped table decorated with Thomas's prize-winning blue and white florals. Expecting a nasty message, I tore open the envelope to find three thousand pounds. She'd returned Fanny's money in full. Maybe there was hope for the wretched woman after all. I slipped the card and money into my purse, wanting to explain the open envelope to the couple.

Declan strolled up behind me, slipping his arms around my waist, placing a warm kiss to my shoulder. Goose bumps skittered across my skin, and I relaxed against him.

"I can't wait until tonight," he whispered in my ear.

My smile grew wider.

We'd graciously given up our room for my aunts and other out-of-town guests, insisting on staying at a nearby inn, along with Zoe and Carrig.

I turned toward Declan, his arms still wrapped around me. "So nice of us to take one for the team, isn't it?"

He slipped a finger under my dress's spaghetti strap and traced it along my shoulder. "Speaking of team, I suppose we should be joining the others." He gave me a teasing kiss, and my heart did a little tap dance.

We walked over to my family gathered around the bartender pouring champagne. Mom wore a long navy dress. Dottie a pastel-blue tea-length one. Teri a short sapphire-colored one. Except for the same bright-blue Irish eyes, Mom and her sisters were as different as Rachel and me. I could sum them up in one salad. Aunt Dottie once forgot to buy tuna fish for our traditional Fourth of July tuna salad. She'd made the dish anyway, hoping nobody would notice. Once short a half teaspoon of salt, Mom apologized to everyone who'd complimented her salad. Aunt Teri was the first to point out the missing ingredients in both salads, despite the fact that she'd brought deli coleslaw to our family gatherings.

"Now that I have most of you here, I want your opinion on the hen party," Mom said.

I held a nervous breath.

"I know afternoon tea might sound a bit boring…"

No, not tea. Nobody had wanted afternoon tea.

Mom peered around at us. "But what if it's in London with Kate, Duchess of Cambridge?"

Fanny and I gasped.

"She's holding a fundraiser." Mom was ready to burst with excitement. "It's a bit pricey, but for a great cause. And we could spend the night in London."

"Such an event could never be too pricey." Fanny placed a hand to her chest, smiling at George. "Just when I thought this day couldn't get any better." She glanced at my mom and aunts. "And I'm so honored to have worn your mother's brooch." She massaged a finger over the silver pin with emerald stones. "Something old, something new." She swept a hand down her long blue lace dress. "Something Irish…" She gazed lovingly at George.

"And everything blue." George smiled, gesturing to his blue vest and cummerbund.

I couldn't wait to give the couple their wedding gift from Declan and me. I'd had Grandma and Michael Daly's engagement photo matted in a double frame with a spot for Fanny and George's wedding pic. Both women had worn the heirloom that was now a wedding-day family tradition.

"We have Caity to thank for bringing us together for such a joyous occasion," Mom said. "Not only has she given me closure with our mother, she's given us a brother and cousins." She smiled at George, then over at Sadie and Seamus.

"Was quite surprised when I received Caity's letter," Sadie told Mom. "Who'd have thought our mums had been corresponding all those years without us having known?"

Mom smiled, no lingering signs of resentment or bitterness toward her mother.

"Now isn't everyone glad I'm a hoarder and kept our mom's letters and naturalization papers?" Teri said. "Who'd have thought they'd one day lead us here."

"To our brother's estate in England," Dottie said.

"*Our* estate," George said. "Thanks to Rachel's and Caity's unwavering determination and efforts, the home will stay in our family for many generations to come."

Rachel gave me a proud smile. "And thanks to Caity's perseverance, she will be bringing families like us together for years."

"Thank heavens for that." Emily placed a loving hand on Liam's arm.

A year ago, I never dreamed I'd go from dressing up as an elf and a sausage to being a genealogist.

The bartender distributed flutes of champagne. After several emotional toasts, and on the verge of tears, I excused myself. Declan followed and slipped a tissue from his pocket. I blew my nose and dabbed at my tears, having cried off most of my eye makeup during the ceremony.

Emily and Liam joined us.

"Not to make you any more emotional, luv, but I must thank you again for putting me in touch with my grandson."

Liam nodded. "I'm flying home next week, hoping to convince my mother to return with me to Ireland to reconcile with my grandma."

"I can't blame her if she refuses," Emily said. "I'm just so happy that I have found my grandson." She gazed at me, teary-eyed. "I don't know how I'll ever thank you enough."

"I just happened to be in the right place at the right time."

"Well, I think it is the right *place* for you and Declan," Emily said. "When I told my son about the home improvements, he was worried I was wasting my money. He confessed to not wishing to hurt my feelings, but neither he nor the children care to own the place. And Liam plans to be a world traveler. I'm hoping you might consider it. I'd give you a marvelous deal."

Excitement zipped through me, my gaze darting to Declan. He gave me a smile and a questioning look.

"I'll have some bonus money I can put toward a down payment. Not sure how much."

He nodded. "Money from the sale of my house should be a good chunk of the payment." He gave me a cautious look. "Of course, this is a joint venture."

I smiled. "I have no problem with you making the down payment."

Declan grasped hold of my hand, lacing our fingers together, his skin warm against mine. I'd never dreamed I'd live in the Daly house, let alone *own* it. But I felt Grandma would approve and want to let bygones be bygones. She'd have adored her husband's sister, Emily. Maybe I'd given Grandma closure by bringing the two families together and now watching over the Coffey home, forever.

"That's simply marvelous," Emily said. "We will work out the details this next week." She excused herself with Liam.

"How perfect is this?" I told Declan. "Her place already feels like home."

"It could feel even more like *our* home." Declan slipped a small blue velvet box from his black suit jacket. He opened it, revealing a silver ring with two hands clasping a crowned heart with an emerald in the middle.

A Claddagh ring—the traditional Irish wedding ring.

My breath caught in my throat.

Was Declan proposing?

"The heart represents love. The hands friendship. The crown loyalty. I promise ya all of this and much more."

My eyes watered, and a lump of emotion in my throat prevented me from yelling out *Yes!*

Declan shifted his stance, a nervous look in his eyes. "Right, then. We can be having a long engagement..."

I shook my head. "I'd say let's elope tonight so I don't have to plan a thing. However, I don't think that would go over well. Getting married at the Daly Estate is now a family tradition. But let's wait to tell everyone. This is Fanny and George's day."

"That was bloody beautiful," Zoe said. "I can't believe we're going to be sisters." She released Carrig's hand and propelled herself toward us for a group hug, causing the ring box to fly from Declan's hand.

Mac snatched up the box and took off across the lawn.

Declan let out a sharp whistle. "Mac! Come back here!"

I knew we couldn't make it through the day without a mishap. But rather than heading for the woods, the ring never to be seen again, Mac circled around, running back toward us.

"Wow, somebody has been busy dog training," Zoe said.

I smiled. "It certainly wasn't me."

Mac returned and dropped the box on the ground at Declan's feet, the ring amazingly still inside it. Declan picked up the box and gave the dog a pat on the head.

"That was a neat trick," Rachel said, walking up. She gasped at the ring box. "Omigod." Her gaze darted to me, and I nodded. "Congratulations!" My sister hugged the life out of me. "I was coming to tell you guys Fanny is getting ready to toss the bouquet. I guess you no longer need to catch it since you'll soon be throwing your own."

I placed a hushing finger to my lips. "We aren't telling anyone yet."

Rachel zipped pinched fingers across her closed lips. She looked at Zoe. "Want to catch a bouquet?"

"Think it'll be a bit before I'm ready to be taking that step," Zoe said.

Carrig nodded in agreement. "We need a few more proper dates, I'd say."

Declan smiled with approval, no snarky remark.

Another proud girlfriend moment.

Rachel pushed her way to the front of the group of single women. Fanny tossed the bouquet over her shoulder. Bypassing the women altogether, it flew toward Gerry's head. His hands shielding his face, he caught the bouquet. The women gave him the evil eye, except for Rachel. She ran up and threw her arms around his neck, kissing him.

The wedding photographer gathered us up for a family portrait in front of the redbrick mansion. Declan and I stood in the center, Mac sitting obediently at our feet. Declan slipped an arm around my waist. I gazed into his dreamy blue eyes, a light flutter tickling my chest. A feeling I knew would last forever.

Standing on a ladder, the photographer tweaked our positions. "Your family gets much bigger, you won't all fit in one snap."

Everyone smiled, knowing our family would grow for years to come.

A year ago I'd been practically estranged from family because of my relationship with my ex. Now I was surrounded by extended family I'd never have discovered if I hadn't taken that first trip to Dublin, trying to escape my life. Luckily, it hadn't taken a million frequent flyer miles to find myself as I'd feared it would.

All the time I'd thought I'd been running from my past, I'd actually been running toward my future.

Available Now in Ebook and Paperback

Learn About Genealogy Research

New Genealogy Mystery Series

Author's Note

Thank you so much for reading *When in Doubt Don't Chicken Out*. If you enjoyed Caity's adventures, I would greatly appreciate you taking the time to leave a review. Reviews encourage potential readers to give my stories a try, and I would love to hear your thoughts. My monthly newsletter features genealogy research advice, my latest news, and frequent giveaways. You can subscribe at www.elizawatson.com.

Thanks a mil!

ABOUT ELIZA WATSON

When Eliza isn't traveling for her job as an event planner, or tracing her ancestry roots through Ireland, she is at home in Wisconsin working on her next novel. She enjoys bouncing ideas off her husband, Mark, and her cats, Frankie and Sammy.

Connect with Eliza Online

www.elizawatson.com

www.facebook.com/ElizaWatsonAuthor

www.instagram.com/elizawatsonauthor